The Trail of Nenaboozhoo

of

Nenaboozhoo

and Other Creation Stories

6th printing

Published by Kegedonce Press
11 Park Road
Neyaashiinigmiing, ON N0H 2T0
www.kegedonce.com
Administration Office/Book Orders
P.O. Box 517
Owen Sound, ON N4K 5R1

Printed in Canada by Gilmore Printing
Edited by: Christi Belcourt
Cover artwork: Isaac Murdoch
Illustrations and artwork:
Isaac Murdoch and Christi Belcourt
Author's photo: Alex Usquiano
Design: Chantal Lalonde Design

Anishinaabemowin is an oral language with many variations in grammar and spelling. The sections that appear here are translations based on the interpretations of Anishinaabe elders, to whom we are extremely grateful. Miigwetch!

Anishinaabemowin Translations: Mary Elizabeth Wemigwans, Linda Toulouse, Mawla Shawana, Howard Webkamigad with assistance from Jessica Shonias, Christi Belcourt, Mary Anne Corbiere, Janet Solomon and Albert Owl.

Library and Archives Canada Cataloguing in Publication

Title: The trail of Nenaboozhoo and other creation stories / Bomgiizhik
   (Isaac Murdoch); Christi Belcourt.
Names: Bomgiizhik, 1975- author, illustrator. | Belcourt, Christi, illustrator, editor.
Description: Some stories in English only. Most stories in Anishinaabemowin
   translation with original English on facing page.
Identifiers: Canadiana 2019018745X | ISBN 9781928120193 (softcover)
Subjects: LCSH: Creation—Folklore. | LCSH: Indigenous peoples—Canada—
   Folklore.
Classification: LCC E99.C6 B66 2019 | DDC 398.2089/97333—dc23

For Customer Service/Orders
Tel 1–800–591–6250 Fax 1–800–591–6251
100 Armstrong Ave. Georgetown, ON L7G 5S4
Email orders@litdistco.ca or visit www.kegedonce.com
We acknowledge the support of the Canada Council for the Arts which last year invested $20.1 million in writing and publishing throughout Canada.

The Canada Council | Le Conseil des Arts
FOR THE ARTS | DU CANADA
SINCE 1957 | DEPUIS 1957

We would like to acknowledge funding support from the Ontario Arts Council, an agency of the Government of Ontario.

ONTARIO ARTS COUNCIL
CONSEIL DES ARTS DE L'ONTARIO
50 YEARS OF ONTARIO GOVERNMENT SUPPORT OF THE ARTS
50 ANS DE SOUTIEN DU GOUVERNEMENT DE L'ONTARIO AUX ARTS

Dedicated
to my beautiful daughter
Waabigwan

CONTENTS

FOREWORD

Stories have shaped my life. The stories I carry, some of which I have put in this book, were told me by various Anishinaabek Elders along the North shores of Lake Huron and Lake Superior. As a child I remember hearing stories from old people at ceremonies and these memories stayed with me vividly and I couldn't stop thinking about them. As a child this led me to want to learn more and to hear more. So, I began to actively seek the stories of my people out.

My journey for a good story has taken me all over the Great Lakes and beyond. I have made offerings for the stories I carry and the stories told in this book and I always followed our ways using our good manners, which means we never take a story or use it without asking and we always give something for it in exchange. This is the Anishinaabek way.

I don't know which one led to the other, but fascination with Ojibwe pictographs always led me to stories and stories often led me to Ojibwe pictographs. And what I learned is that there is no separation between the people, the land and the spirits that live here. This world is a magical place and is the home of Little People, Thunderbirds, Serpents and mysterious forest dwellers. As we lived our life on the land we zigzagged through their homes making sure to give offerings for having such a beautiful place to stay. I always feel like I'm a guest in such amazing company. The land is our stories and the stories help teach us how to live on it. This knowledge is not my knowledge, but knowledge from the land that was passed down by Elders and knowledge keepers of the past.

I am Ojibwe, I belong to the Fish Clan and I come from Serpent River First Nation. We reside on the North Shore of Lake Huron. Historically we have always been a hunting and gathering people that has had close ties to the land. My people had the Anishinaabe education and knowledge to live their lives without ever using a garbage can. Their high discipline of Anishinaabe education allowed them to pass down sustainable non-intrusive economies for thousands of generations without leaving a footprint. This is something western education has not been able to provide. And so, it's always with great excitement and honour to be able to hear stories and teachings that were passed down from our Elders. These are truly the greatest gifts I have ever received from my people. Our world view stems from the land, our language and our connection to all living beings. Colonization, the Indian Act, and the colonial treaties have caused separation from the land for many of our people.

We are a land people. This is our history. I feel it's important that we reclaim who we are as Indigenous People and take our rightful place back in the forests where we come from. As long as we have our language and our land we will never be conquered, we will never disappear, and we will never fully be dissolved into colonial society. Right now, our people are fighting back and they are winning due to language revitalization and land-based learning. These two go hand in hand in the development of our people. Our true governance stems from the fire and the waters and all the mystery and magic that surrounds it.

Nenaboozhoo left us many gifts.

Everything we have can be accredited to the gifts from the spirit world. As we are now in abrupt climate change we can see the world-wide ecological collapse happening before our very eyes. How important was the birch bark canoe? The wigwam? How important were those gifts that were given to us? I think they were very important. They were more than important, they were sacred.

And so, it's with great hopes and encouragement that I offer these stories as a map to understand how to go back to the old ways. The old people always said we are going to go back to the old ways and I truly believe the time is now. We musn't wait.

Nenaboozhoo is a spirit that was brought to the earth who is highly respected to this day by my people. They say when he was in spirit form, he went through four levels of power. Through each power he went through he went back to the centre saying he didn't want to leave. But the Great Mystery told him, "Keep going, keep going, you're needed somewhere."

And he made his way through those four powers and ended up on earth. His life here on earth was magical. All the rivers, all of the moutains, all of the beautiful colours that we see, were created with Nenaboozhoo and his magical trail on earth. They say one day ten men will go fasting and call Nenaboozhoo back and the world will be new again. Nothing can stop the power that is here.

The Birth of Nenaboozhoo

When I was growing up, from as long as I can remember, I heard my Elders speak about Nenaboozhoo. Whenever the elders saw a whirlwind, they would often say, "There is Nenaboozhoo." Or they would say "Nenaboozhoo is in that rock over there, hiding." Or they would see a rabbit, "Oh there's Nenaboozhoo." Or they would see something really spectacular, maybe a bird they never saw before, or a pure white animal and say, "Oh there's Nenaboozhoo."

I started to think, 'Who is this Nenaboozhoo?' To me he sounded almost like God, or the Creator, or someone very spiritual and strong. I started to ask questions about who Nenaboozhoo was. My Dad had some stories, my grandparents had stories, the elders had stories and I started to realize that all these stories are all just the parts of a bigger story.

There's a bigger story that needs to be told about Nenaboozhoo and it's coded in the land. It's a story about the place names and the names of everything, and the reasons why places or animals or objects carry the names they do. Nenaboozhoo stories are all connected. Many seem not to have any ending, and the next ones appear to pick up where the last ones left off. Each Nenaboozhoo story is just a piece in a large puzzle. I'm not qualified to tell this grand story about Nenaboozhoo, of course. But today I'd like to give you a little insight about what I know about Nenaboozhoo that I have heard from my Elders.

The Elders say Nenaboozhoo often comes in human form as a very striking young warrior. He is very gifted and handsome. He looks real deadly in buckskin. They say that his arrows were perfectly straight, and that these arrows could go right

to the end of the earth if it had to, to kill his enemy. So all of these things I heard started to excite me.

What I also found out was that Nenaboozhoo came from very humble beginnings. He came from, I guess you could say, a 'broken home.' The story of Nenaboozhoo all begins with his grandmother.

They say Nenaboozhoo's grandmother Nokomis lived on the moon and the moon herself was Nokomis' grandmother.

Nokomis lived there with her sisters on her grandmother. And like sisters do, sometimes they fight over silly things. They say Nokomis and her sisters were fighting over a hair piece and then one sister threw Nokomis off the moon. She hurled and twirled as she fell all the way down until she hit the earth and she landed in a lake and sank to the bottom. She sat at the bottom of the lake pouting and thinking about everything. She was so mad at her sister for what she had done just over a hair piece.

Somebody watched her fall from the moon down into the lake and was watching as she sat on the bottom pouting. It was a big old Bear. The Bear was sitting on a rock and he saw everything. But you know how bears are, they are quiet, they just sit there and watch.

After that Bear had sat there for many days, eating his berries and thinking about that beautiful woman at the bottom of the lake, he swam into the lake, putting his head down looking for that woman. Bears are excellent swimmers. Finally he spotted her in the deepest part of the lake and he asked Nokomis, "Why don't you come up here?"

"Oh I'm not going up there" she said. "When I hit the water, my medicine bag opened and all my medicine is at the bottom of the lake. I'm not going up there without my medicine."

Well of course that Bear felt sorry for her, so he kept bugging her, everyday he would go back. "Why don't come up here with me? It's nice and warm up here. It's sunny. It's so dark down here. There's a lot of bad spirits down there that will get you. You should come up here with me." And after a while that must have sounded pretty inviting, because they say she swam to the top of the lake and crawled on that Bear's back. The Bear told her, "Don't worry, maybe one day you will get your medicine back, don't worry about it."

They went to the west side of the lake. They built a beautiful wigwam. The wigwam was like two teepees, but connected, so it looked like a long tipi. There was spruce (Gawaandok) hanging all the way around and beautiful cedar mats, and two fires were lit at either end. Everything was beautiful. Everything was perfect. And that's where they lived. And you know what? They fell in love. They fell in love and they didn't marry because at that time, when you fell in love with

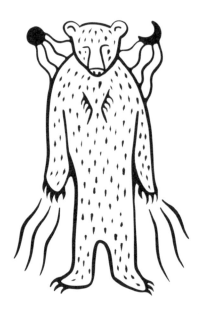

someone you just shacked up with them. So that's what they did, they shacked up in this beautiful wigwam.

Before long, just shortly after, she started to feel something in her belly. She was pregnant. They were going to have a little baby, but something was very different about this; it wasn't just a regular pregnancy. They say that the baby grew very fast, very quickly. Her belly was starting to get very, very big and you could hear thunder and lightning crashing inside. They knew that whatever was in her belly was very powerful.

Nokomis didn't know what was going to happen when she gave birth. They say it was a very beautiful afternoon when she started to have her baby. She gave birth to a tiny little girl and Nokomis named her Winona. The baby was part spirit, and part bear, which is also like a spirit. So even though the baby looked like a regular baby, she was very, very powerful.

The baby grew up quickly and was incredibly beautiful. She grew up to be a very outstanding woman and a hard worker. Her mom put her out to fast every year starting when she was ten years old until she was nineteen. For nine years she put her daughter out to fast for ten days. After her last fast, they knew it was time for her daughter to go and find a husband. Back then, animals and humans could be together. And they say that because she was so beautiful, everyone wanted to be with her.

But of course the one that won her over, they say, was probably the meanest one. It was the West Wind who stole her heart. When they got together her mom didn't like that at all. Her mom said the West Wind was mean and that he would be nice in the beginning, but after a while, she said, "He's probably going to start beating you up." And of course the more her mom tried to dissuade her, the more Winona didn't believe her and wanted to be with the West Wind because he was very powerful as well and many powers come from the West.

Winona shacked up with the West Wind, and shortly after, he started to become violent to her and beat her up just as her mother had warned. When Winona became pregnant, the West Wind left her.

As her belly got big, the same thing that happened to her mother began to happen to her. Thunder and lightning was crashing in her belly. Then as she was giving birth something else was happening too. The waters along the shoreline began to bubble. The Serpents and those beings that live underneath were very scared of what was in her belly. They were scared of that power and they didn't like it because the Serpents' power that comes from below was naturally in conflict with the power that comes from up above from the west.

Winona just didn't have one baby, she had four.

They say the first baby that came out was a baby Rabbit. It was the most powerful of all babies. Nokomis took that

little baby Rabbit that wasn't even developed yet over to the wigwam. She put dry grass on top of the baby to keep it warm and then put a bowl on top of the baby to keep it safe.

Meanwhile, as Nokomis was tending to the first baby in the wigwam, Winona gave birth to her other three babies. This all happened very quickly. The second baby to come was half human and half rabbit. He was eventually named Jiibayaboos. That baby hopped away as soon as it was born.

The third baby to be born was a tiny little human looking baby and they say that lightning was shooting out that baby's mouth and thunder would crash every time it cried. The third baby also took off running. Later on, we find out that this brother comes back to live with Nenaboozhoo when he was a child for a short time.

The fourth and last of Winona's babies was a very difficult birth because this baby was made of rock. This baby was not a smooth stone, but had sharp and jagged edges. Sadly, Winona passed away giving birth to that last baby. And again, this baby rock upon being born, rolled away.

All of this happened so quickly, that by the time Nokomis returned to Winona, she found her daughter had passed away and there were no other babies to be found. This is why Nenaboozhoo was the only grandchild Nokomis had raised.

That is how they say Nenaboozhoo and his brothers came to this world. The baby who had turned into the Rabbit under the cedar bowl was Nenaboozhoo. And so we know that his power is the West Wind because that's who his dad is. We know that he also gets his powers from the stars because that's where his family comes from. We know that his grandpa was that old Bear so Nenaboozhoo had his place on this earth too and it's where he got his gift of medicines from. And because all of those powers were combined in him, it made a hell of a person. It made a very strong person.

Nenaboozhoo grew up with his grandmother Nokomis, and she always put him out to fast. As soon as he was old enough they grabbed cedar coal and rubbed it all over his face and sent him to the mountain. He'd stay there for a long time, until he got his gift that he was waiting for. That's where he got the gift of his arrows that he was so famous for. He got all his gifts from those fasts. Fasting is what his mom Winona went through, it's probably what his grandma went through, and that's what he had to go through. So when he was growing up, he grew up very, very strong. And like most young people, when they have a really special gift, they test it and maybe they even abuse it a little bit, that's how he was too.

When Nenaboozhoo was a young man he asked his grandmother, "How come I've only seen my one brother? Where did the others go? Why are there no people?" Nokomis told him that Windigo had turned all the people into trees. So Nenaboozhoo went to go find Windigo and kill him, which he eventually did and then turned the trees back to humans.

They said that because he had such a strong power, he would go on a war path. And he would come back with many enemy captives. His grandmother would ask him "Why are you doing that? How come you are going on a warpath all the time? Those are your nephews, don't bother them." And she scolded him, as she often did.

Nenaboozhoo replied, "I wish I had a mom to raise me," and the old lady looked at him and said, "I tried my best, but something happened to your mom." And she told him the story of how his mom passed away because he didn't know. This infuriated him. Because he knew that he lost his mom to that last brother born as a jagged stone, he wanted to go find him. That anger lived inside of him, and he decided to go look for his brother to kill him.

This is when Nenaboozhoo went on a long journey to go find his brothers and his dad.

Nenaboozhoo miinwaa Ma'iingan

Nenaboozhoo gii bshigendamaan Anishinaaben gaa zhi zhichigewaad. Gii bshigendaan gaa zhi nookniiyewaad, gaa zhi maadziwaad, miinwaa dash wiinwaa da Dodemowaan, miinwaa aaniish gaa zhi gnawenmowaad Wiigwaaman, gnaajwang miinwaa biinchigaadek. Miinwaa gii bshigendaan gaawiin gii miigaandisiiwag. Gii maamiikwendmaan Anishinaaben gaa zhi maadiwaad.

Wi pii, Anishinaabek gaawiin gii yaaziinaawaa shkode. Mii dash Nenaboozhoo gii wiindamoowaad, "nda nendam ngkendaan eminezyeg nga doowaabmdaan. Giishpin bi bskaabiiswaan, giishpin tpineyaan maanda zhichigeyaan wii biidoowaan maanda, nda ndoowendaan mkwendmiiyeg miinwaa wii ngamyeg Nenaboozhoo ngamwinan."

Nenaboozhoo and the Wolf

Nenaboozhoo really liked the Anishinaabek for the way that they conducted themselves. He liked the way they dressed, the way they lived, how their families were, and how they kept their lodges nice and clean. And he liked that there was no infighting amongst them. He really respected the Anishinaabek for how they were as a nation.

At that time, the Anishinaabek didn't have fire. So Nenaboozhoo told them, "I think I know what you need. I'm going to go look for it. But if I don't come back, if I perish in my quest to bring you this, I want you to remember me and sing songs about me."

Maamwi gii kidawag "na'haaw"

Nenaboozhoo gii zhaa zaagiganing, gii bboong, miinwaa gii waabndaanan niibna mkadewsiing ekwaa'iing jiigbiig mii gii gkendang Maa'iinganag aawaad. Gii ni zhaa miinwaa gii wiijiiwaan giw Maa'iinganag miinwaa gii kwedwe, "gdaa wiijiiwninim na? Ndoo doowaabndaan gegoo wii naadamogwaa nwiiji bemaadiz?"

Wewiip gii kidwag, "Kaa, gaawiin gdaa wiijiiwsiimi, gaawiin gda piichkaasii."

"Noos aawi epingishmok noodin," gii nkwetam, "Ngizhiikaa naasaap epkaanzid."

"Na'haaw, giishpin enendimoone gizhiikaayin miinwaa de piiskaayin, na'haaw dash. Giishpin dash wii go gaawiin gshkitooswan, nshike bmiptoon." Mii dash Nenaboozhoo gii maajii wiijibitoomaad Maa'iinganan.

Mii zhi gii gkendang waa zhi ntaa giiwsed. Maa'iinganan gii kinomaagoon. Kidwag giiyenh, Gimaa Maa'iingan giichi mndida, giichi mkade'ozi, miinwaa giichi mshkodaamkan. Nenaboozhoo gii wiindamowaan Maa'iingan, "Gaawiin nwiiyaasii pane. Gii miizhim gchi niibna. Nda ndoowaabndaan gegoo ge bskaabwid damaagwaa ningonesag."

Gimaa Mahiingan gii kida, "Wegnesh e'paa ndawaamdaman?"

"Shkode waa biidmo gwa neyaap bemaadizijik" gii kida Nenaboozhoo.

They agreed. They said "okay."

Nenaboozhoo went to the lake, and it was wintertime, and he saw several black dots at the edge of the lake, and he knew that they were Wolves. He went and joined those Wolves and asked, "Can I travel with you because I'm trying to find something to help my people?"

Right away they said, "No, you can't come with us because you're not fast enough."

"My dad is the West Wind," he replied, "I'm as fast as anybody."

"Alright if you think you're fast and if you can keep up then by all means. But if you can't, then good luck to you." So Nenaboozhoo started to run with the Wolves.

That is where he learned how to become an expert hunter. He learned from those Wolves. And they say that the Chief Wolf, Ma'ingun was very, very big and very black and had a strong jaw. And Nenaboozhoo told that Wolf, "I can't stay with you forever. You have given me so much but I'm looking for something, I'm looking for something to bring back to my nephews, the Anishinaabek."

The Chief Wolf said, "What is that you're looking for?"

Nenaboozhoo said, "Fire, to bring back to the people."

"Manda aabdek waa zhichigeyin, kwii kodaabidebnaa maaba ningonis." Kida Gimaa Ma'iingan. Mii sa go gaa zhitchiget Nenaboozhoo.

"Siniing bizikaamigat nmashkoziiwin." Kidawan ningonisan.

"Wegnesh sin?" gii kida Nenaboozhoo

"Wi menjigoniman." Gii kida Gimaa Ma'iingan

Ga na bit Nenaboozhoo ninjiihn mii gii waabndang niish skaaknes'jiganan tenik.

"Bezhig iw sin wii boodweyin, wi dash bezhik wii zhitooyin gdoo bikwokoon." Gii kida Ma'iingan.

The Wolf Chief then said, "Here is what you have to do. You have to reach your hand into my nephew's mouth and pull out his tooth." So Nenaboozhoo did.

The nephew said, "My power comes from that stone."

Nenaboozhoo said, "What stone?"

The Wolf Chief said, "The one you have in your hand."

Nenaboozhoo looked in his hand and there were two pieces of flint in his hand.

The Wolf said, "The one rock is for fire, the other is for your arrows."

Ma'iingan ningonisan gii gchimbagwaashkoninit. Waasa ge'e giizhik washkonewan. Pii gaa tkokiisenit, mii zowaanikong gii zaagidakonesenit mii giiska'aget.

Wi nji gwetaaninegatchtoo'yin gegoo miinwaa aapji minadodeman gdaa daapanaa ningonis wii wiikaaneyin, dinaan Gimaa Ma'iingan Nenboozhoo'in. "Mewzha, gii bi tibijiise mkade sin. Binoojiinhs gii aawi. Ngii kooginaanaa wii debendmengit. Gii aanjnaawgozi maa'iinganing gii bi zh'naawgozi. Gii wiijigendaawgonaa."

Gaawiin gii-gkendanziin Nenaboozhoo wiikaaneyin aawnit gaa-daapinaajin, niw bebaandawaamaapniin wii-nsaat. Gchinendam gii mkowaad sa'yeyan aapji gaa zaagaajin miinwaa gaa manaadendamaajin gaawiin gii gshkitoosiin wii nsaad.

Ma'iingan miinwaa nenaboozhoo maamwi gii-paayaawag. Gii waabmiigaazwag ko aapiichin.

The Wolf's nephew then jumped very high and long way, and when he landed sparks came out of his tail and they landed on some brush and it started a fire. Nenaboozhoo knew that that gift of flint is very strong. He wanted to get back to the Anishinaabek to give them this priceless gift.

The Wolf Chief told Nenaboozhoo, "Because you're so outstanding, because you're very polite, you get to adopt my nephew to be your brother. Many years ago, a black stone rolled into our camp. It was only a baby. We raised it to be our own, and it turned into a Wolf to live with us."

So, it was then Nenaboozhoo realized that was his brother who he had been on a quest to find and kill. He loved and respected the wolf so much he couldn't kill him and he was instead happy to have found his brother.

Nenaboozoo and his brother became travelling partners, and they often were seen together.

Nenaboozhoo and the Serpents

One day something happened to Nenaboozhoo's brother the Wolf. Nenaboozhoo told him, "Never go on the lake in the winter time, because those spirits that live underneath are jealous of me and my power. If they see you on the lake, maybe they'll get you and kill you."

Shkode-sin-inini thought, 'Maybe he is just saying that, thinking that if I go on the lake, I'll get homesick and just go back to my people. But I will never leave him, that's my brother. But I still want to go on the lake and run around.'

So of course the Wolf went to the lake and right away
the ice cracked open and the Serpents went and grabbed
Nenaboozhoo's brother. They brought him to the very bottom
and they ripped him to pieces. The Wolf was gone. And they
say that the only thing left was his head. The Serpents took
the Wolf's head and threw it up on the shoreline and they say
it's still there to this day.

Nenaboozhoo was furious and decided to go to war with the
Serpents.

The Serpents are not something you fool around with. They
say that the Serpents have big horns and arms and legs,
they're strong and fast swimmers, they can move quickly
on land as well. We know that those Serpents have a power
that's much greater than ours. But Nenaboozhoo didn't care,
all he could think about was to kill them.

One day the Serpents were laying on the beach soaking up
sun. Nenaboozhoo hid himself by turning into a stump. And
then when they weren't looking, the stump would move
over to get a little bit closer. Meanwhile they didn't know
that the stump was there because they were not even paying
attention. The stump was getting closer and closer and before
long, that stump was just right beside them on the beach.

Nenaboozhoo waited for them to look away one last time and
when they did, he jumped out with his arrows, and started to
shoot the Serpents. He killed all of them except one. With the
last Serpent he cut off its nose and horns and said, "You go
back and tell the other Serpents that if they want more I got
it!" —and he sent that last Serpent back down.

As expected the water started to bubble and all those
Serpents that found out what Nenaboozhoo did were enraged
with him. The Serpents decided that they had to kill him,

and they had to kill him quick. So they hired someone to kill Nenaboozhoo.

This hired assassin wasn't just a regular person. She was a very powerful Old Lady who could turn into a tiny little Frog. The Serpents gave that Frog a very powerful medicine at the end of her tongue. They said that all the Frog had to do was lick Nenaboozhoo once and he would perish because that's how powerful the medicine was.

Nenaboozhoo was sitting there one day and all of a sudden a little Frog comes bouncing along, but that Frog didn't even know it was Nenaboozhoo.

The Frog said, "Hey I'm looking for Nenaboozhoo."

Nenaboozhoo said, "I don't know where he is, I heard he is out west somewhere. I have no idea where he went."

"Oh okay," said the Frog.

Nenaboozhoo asked, "How come you are looking for Nenaboozhoo?"

"Well I don't know," said the Frog, reluctant to tell the man her business.

Nenaboozhoo was smart and he told that little frog, "I don't like him, if you find him let him know that I want to fight him."

Nenaboozhoo tricked the frog and the little Frog said, "You know what? Me too!" She continued, "I want to kill him too. I've been employed by the Serpents to kill him. Maybe we can kill him together?"

Nenaboozhoo said, "Yeah maybe we can."

As soon as that Frog turned around, Nenaboozhoo grabbed
his arrow and stabbed that Frog and killed her. The little Frog
didn't have a chance; it was over before it started because
Nenaboozhoo was smart.

He said to himself, "I'm going to turn myself into that Frog,
and I'm going to go down there and kill the Serpents with
their own poison."

So Nenaboozhoo took the Frog and cut it open and then
wrapped the Frog's skin around his own body and went down
as an imposter pretending to be that Old Lady.

Now that he was the Frog, Nenaboozhoo had his chance to go
down to where the Serpents were, so he jumped into the lake
and he started to swim downward. When he got down there
the Serpents thought he was the little Frog coming to report
to them and they asked her, "So how did it go?"

"Oh I killed him! That medicine worked! Nenaboozhoo is dead!"

The Serpents said, "Good! Good! Good!" They were happy and started to celebrate.

As soon as the Serpents looked away, Nenaboozhoo turned into his human form and shot them all with his arrows. But they say he never shot them in their body, he shot them in their shadow.

They say that the Anishinaabe is made up of three parts. You always hear four, but when I was younger I always heard three. There is the physical body, there is the spirit, and there is the shadow. The shadow is often overlooked but it's a part of us.

After he killed the Serpents Nenaboozhoo swam to the top of the lake and he saw a Bird there.

The Bird said, "Boy you're pretty good, you got powerful medicine. But I've been watching everything. I've been watching the whole drama of you guys for a long time now. And Nenaboozhoo maybe you killed this little tribe here, but this lake is filled with them all over. And they're going to get you."

Nenaboozhoo said, "Why are you talking to me like that?" He said, "Take that back."

This colourful bird said, "No."

Nenaboozhoo said, "Because you said that, I'm going to take all your colours away and put them in my bag." That bird today is known as Aandeg (the Crow).

Nenaboozhoo miinwaa Gchi-mooshka'ang

Nenaboozhoo e ni giiwed endaanid, gii noondaawaan wiyaa nshiinajigwaad Okomisan maa wiigwaaming. Wiyaa doo shinaandenmaan nokmisaan, gii nendaam. Gii gwaansigendaam. Gii zhi bmowaan, zhaabi wigwaaming, gii miikwaan, mkwaa gaabi zaagjibawed. Gaawiin gii kendmaasiin omishomsan aawnid, niiw mkwaan, aanwi go naa pane gii aanji-aanjnaagoze epiichi kog'nind.

Nenaboozhoo gii bmiinaashkowaan, gii ni dimnewaan, gii nsaan, gii biiskwanaan, wii shkobziwaad. Epiichi shkobziged, gii maamninaabmaan mtigoon e mede aazhdeaakshinwaad, gii zhiingtawaan. Gii kwadandwe'aanaan mtigoon wii waa gdiskbinaad shpiming, wii bwaa mde'aakoshkaanig. Wiin dash gii baataashin.

Epiichi baataashing maa; wagoshenyan gii bigamoodmigoon, kina gii maajiiptwaa-daanaawaa wiiyaasim. Mii go eta mkwa shtigwan gaa shkwanmoowaad.

Gegpii sa gii shkwaa baataashin. Gwetaangidaazo. Ginebigoonsing gii zhi aanjidzo. Gii biindoode biinji mkwa dooning, shtigwaaning, kina gegoo gii miijin. Kina gegoo gii miijin, owiinendip, oshkiinzhigoon, miinwaa odeniw. Kina gegoo gii miijin.

Nenaboozhoo and the Great Flood

Nenaboozhoo went back home to Nookomis and heard sexual noises coming from the wigwam. He thought someone was taking advantage of his grandmother. He was infuriated. So he shot his arrow through the wigwam and wounded someone inside and out came a Bear who took off running. He didn't know the Bear was his grandpa because he had always shape-shifted into a man while raising him.

Nenaboozhoo chased the Bear down and killed it and cut it up into pieces and then he started to smoke it. While he was smoking it, he noticed these two trees that were crossed and rubbing against each other, making a squeaking noise and it was irritating him. So he climbed those trees to go bust them off at the top so they wouldn't make that noise. But he got stuck between those trees.

While he was stuck there a whole bunch of foxes came and grabbed all his meat and took off with it. The only thing that was left was that Bear's head.

Finally he got unstuck. He was mad. He turned himself into a little snake. He crawled into the Bear's mouth, into his head and started to eat what he could out of it. He started to eat its brain, its eyes, its tongue. He was eating everything.

Gnebigoonswid gii gshkitoon wii baamooded biinji mkwa
shtigwan. Epiichi wiisnid Nenaboozhoo minwaa epiichi
migotaad , gii ni maajiibde shtigwaan jiige-giishkaapkaag.
Epiichi wiisnid, eshkam gwa gii ni gzhiibde tetibisenh mkwa
shtigwaan , tkami akiing , gweyak sa gwa giishkaapkaag.
Niisaa'ing giishkaabkaag temgat waanzh, naaminibi
njimnidook endaawaad. Gii njibde, naam zaagigan, biinish gii
ni biinjibideg waanzhiing, naambi mnidook endaawaad,

Migoo wewiip naambi mnidook gii gwejimaad ginebigoonsan
"giin na Nenaboozhoo?"

"Kaa, ngikenmaa sa gwa eyaad" gii kida

Miigwa gaa zhi giibaasmaad gii gkendmaad gii aanid
mnidoon ntaa giibaazige maaba Nenaboozhoo. Aapji gii
gchi mamiikwendimook, gii booni kwaamdamaazwag.
Nenaboozhoo gii bskaabi aanji naagozi, mii dash gii maajii
baashkizowaad kina naambii gawaateshing mnidook, niibna
gii nsaan. Gii gshkitoon maanda wii zichiged, aabjitood wi
mshomisan omshkiim. Onji mishoomsan gii nji miigaazo, gii
pkinaage dash.

Gaa gwa chi-wiikaa, wa Chi-Gimaa Ginebig, gii
nkweshkodaadwaad ndaamaawaad kina naaminbi mnidoog.
Gii giizhendmook wii aabjitowaad mshkikiimwaa wii
moshkamwaad aki wii gzowbowinaawaad Nenaboozhoon. Mii
gaa zhi moshko'ojikaamwaad aki.

Ngoding giizigak gii maajii moshka'an. Gaawiin gii
gmiweziinoon, gii maajii moska'an eta. Gii giidakii'ewak gchi-
aazhibikoong, wii zhaabwiiwaad, wii bemaadziwaad. Kina
wesiihyak ge'e wiinwaa gii zhaawak chi-aazhibikoong. Ge'e
wiin gwaa Nenaboozhoo.

As a little snake, he began rolling around inside that Bear's head eating. Nenaboozhoo kept eating and twirling around and that head just kept rolling towards that cliff. As he ate, it created a momentum and that Bear's head started to roll slowly across the land right towards the big cliff. On the bottom of that cliff was a lake with a big tunnel in it where Serpents lived. It rolled right off, right into the lake, directly into that Serpent tunnel and that head sunk right to the bottom and it landed in the land of Serpents.

Right away the Serpent started to question the little snake, "are you Nenaboozhoo?"

Nenaboozhoo said, "No, but I know where he is!"

Nenaboozhoo was such a smooth talker he convinced those Serpents that he knew where he was. And they got all joyous and they let their guard down. Nenaboozhoo turned himself into human form and started to shoot all those Serpents' shadows again killing lots of them. He was able to do that using his grandpa's power. The nourishment for that battle came from his grandpa and he was victorious.

Shortly after, the Chief of the Serpents called a meeting with all of the Serpents. It was agreed they were going to use their medicine to flood the earth to drown Nenaboozhoo. That is how they began to flood the earth.

One day the water began to rise. It didn't rain, the water just rose and rose. Everybody was trying to live, just trying to survive, so they started to climb to the mountain tops. All the animals were on top of the mountains. And Nenaboozhoo was up there too.

Eshkam gwa gii ni mooshka'an, Nenaboozhoo gii maajii kwaandawe mtigoong. Pii e ni dimnegwad nibiish, gii maajii ngaamo, mshkikii ngaamwin, epiitaandwed gwa gii ni maajiigi mtig. Eshkam dash gwa gii ni mooshka'an. Pii e ni dimnegwad nibiish miinwaa, Nenaboozhoo gii ngamo bekaanag mshkikii ngamowin, Miinwa gii majiigi bangii mtig. Giiyaabi gwa eshkam gii mooshka'an. Eko nsing ngamowin miinwaa, Nenaboozhoo gii ngamo, pii e ni dimnegwad nibiish. Eko niizhing, miinwaa gii majiige mtig, bangii eta. O'dooning gwa gii ni kwa mooshka'ani.

'Megwaa maamik naaminibi mnidook wii gwaanaabaaw'izhiwaad, wii bkinwizh'waad' gii nendam , e ni piichi mooshka'ang.

Geskanaa gii shkwaa mooshka'an, mii Nenaboozhoo gii gkendan eko nsiing ngamowin gii nokiimgag. Mii sa aanwi, gii gwonaabaawa'naawaad gii nendmook naaminibi mnidook.

As the water was rising, Nenaboozhoo began to climb a tree. When the water reached his body, Nenaboozhoo sang a medicine song and the tree grew taller. But the water kept rising. When it reached his body again Nenaboozhoo sang another medicine song. This time the tree grew again, but not as much as the first time. The water kept rising. When it reached his body again, Nenaboozhoo sang a third song. This time the tree grew a little, but not as much as the second time. The water kept rising until it rose right up to his mouth.

He was thinking to himself as the water was rising, 'The Serpents are actually going to drown me, they actually won.'

Right at that moment, the water stopped rising, and Nenaboozhoo knew that his third song had worked. And surely by then the Serpents had thought that he had been killed.

Geyaabi gwa gii nese, maa nmadbid maamoonji gnoosid mtig, maa maamoonji shpidinak. Gaawaanh gii nji zhaabwii. Gii gkendaan gegoo aabdek wii zhichiged. Niibna Anishnaabeg gii nbowag, gii chi-mooshka'ang.

'Aabdek gwa gegoo wii nda zhichigeyaanh, aabdek gwa Aki wii bskaabwidmowgwaa Anishnaabeg gaa zhaabwiijg.' Nenaboozhoo gii nendam.

Nenaboozhoo gii kwejmaan bebkaan wesiinhyan da naajigogiitamowaad Aki. Niibnaa bneshiinhyag gii gwejtoon naa waa. Miinwaa gwa pkaan wesiinhyag. Zaam gii goniindmaa, gii bskaabiiwag, gii noonde naamwag. Mii sa ozhaashk gii kida wii zhaad.

Nenaboozhoo gii debinan ozhaashkwan wii nesetwaad. Gii mooshka'an nesewin jibwaa gogiinid. Gii gshkitoon gwa wii debidood bangii aki, gii noondese dash nodin jibwaa mookset. Gii noonde gwanaabaawe, gii mooshkaangjise, tkwanang iwi Aki.

Nenaboozhoo gii bagosendaan chi-Aki-shkiwewsiwin, miinwa osayeyan Maa'iingan wiibe naadmaagwad. Gii debidoon Aki, gii boodaadaan,mii dash gii maajii Akiimgag. Gii maajiigin Aki. Ma'iingaan ogii naagadoon Aki,shaawe'ii epiichiging enso giizhgag aaniish miinig gaa maajiishkaag. Mii 'iw nendam, Nenaboozhoo, e nii giizhgag, niiwin.

Nenaboozhoo gii pskaabwidoon Aki, wii eyaawaad gaa zhaabwiijig Anishnaabeg miinwaa wesiinhyag. Wesiinhyen gii naadmaagoon wii zhitoowad ziibiin, zaagaginan, aazhbikoong miinwaa mtigoog. Kinaa gegoo gii zhiitoonaawaa. Gii gnaajiwan. Gii chi nokiiwag.

There sat Nenaboozhoo at the top of the tallest mountain, on the tallest tree still sucking air. He had barely made it. He knew that he had to do something. And at that time when those Serpents flooded the earth, a lot of Anishinaabek perished.

Some Anishinaabek survived by being tough, so Nenaboozhoo thought, 'I have to do something. I have to bring the land back to the people.'

Nenaboozhoo started to ask the different Animals that were around to swim down to the bottom of the waters and bring up some earth. Many Birds tried. And different Animals. But they ran out of air before they could get to the bottom, so they swam back up. So Muskrat said he would go.

Nenaboozhoo grabbed the Muskrat and blew into its mouth. He filled him up with air and sent him down. Muskrat made it and was able to grab a handful of earth but ran out of air coming up. He died and floated to the top, and in his hand was the dirt.

Nenaboozhoo spoke to the powers of the universe and asked for his brother the Wolf to come down and help him. And he grabbed that dirt and he blew it and it started to create land. The land just started to grow. The Wolf followed the land, he followed the edge of it as it was growing and reported back every day how far it was. On the fourth day Nenaboozhoo thought that was enough.

Nenaboozhoo had brought back the land for the surviving animals and humans. With his helpers, the Animals, they created the rivers, the lakes, the mountains, and the trees. They created everything. It was beautiful. They worked hard at it.

Nenaboozhoo Creates the Spirit World

Nenaboozhoo noticed that all the spirits who perished during the Great Flood were just roaming aimlessly in the sky with nowhere to rest, and he thought, 'I think I know what to do.' Noticing that a Turtle was pouting by a rock, Nenaboozhoo said, "Why don't you do me a favour, you're so beautiful and you're so gifted, why don't you bring me some nice beautiful stones from the edge of the lake 'cause I want to use them." The Turtle was mad because when Nenaboozhoo was creating the earth he didn't include Turtle, so Turtle was jealous and he felt left out. As the Turtle was at the edge of the lake, Nenaboozhoo grabbed him and threw him far out into the lake. The Turtle was very angry and swam to the bottom and sat right in the middle of the lake. When that Turtle came up for air Nenaboozhoo shot his arrow at it, and of course that arrow hit that shell and when it did, startled Turtle and all the mud that had gathered from the bottom of the lake on the Turtle's back and tail flipped up into the sky. And they say it created Jibiiy Miikan, the sacred path in the afterlife that went from East to West.

The mud that was on Turtle's back and tail had come from Nenaboozhoo's grandmother Nokomis's medicine that was all scattered at the bottom of the lake. It was her medicine that got flung right across the sky.

Nenaboozhoo knew that, and when he saw it he said, "This is a sacred trail and to finish this I'm going to make a place for those who departed." Nenaboozhoo walked down the path that goes from East to West, and at the end he created the spirit world.

They say he was there for a long time creating everything and he made it very beautiful, even more beautiful than the earth. All of the rocks were gorgeous, the trees, the animals and their colours were absolutely pure.

So that's how the spirit world came to the Anishinaabek. They say that when someone passes away, their spirits go through the Eastern Door, and they travel South and out the Western Door. And they say that his brother, Jiibayaboos, the brother that was born as half human and half rabbit, wanted to look after that place up there. So Nenaboozhoo told his brother, "I will send you there, and that will be your place to look after."

Jiibayaboos to became the keeper of the path of souls that we call the Jiibiy Miikan (the Milky Way). You will often see Jiibayaboos and his brother the Wolf on the road, and our people know to call upon them during the times of their death ceremonies.

The Anishinaabek always believe that when we travel that road, that it's very sacred, but it's also very dangerous. They say that since the spirit world was created, there are tests of bravery and strength. One of the tests they say, is that when you reach into that Doorway, the very first thing you come across is a path in the spirit world that travels West.

The first person you meet as you start your journey is a spirit named Niigaaninini who sits at the Doorway where you enter the next world. He will show how to get to Jiibiy Miikan. Once you follow that path you will meet an Old Lady at a split in the

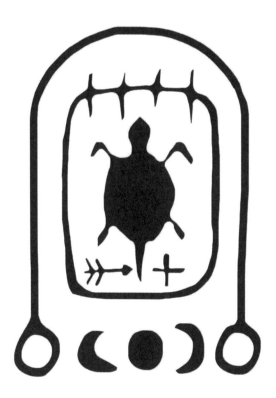

road. And she will ask you, "Which way are you going to go? Are you going to go this way, or that way? You have to pick."

And they say at that time, your soul will have to put down tobacco, to try to guess, to understand which way to go. And once you put your tobacco down you will know.

Once you are there you will see a big strawberry on your left, you will know you are on the right path. You are not to eat that strawberry.

Then you will travel along that path once more, and you will meet a bunch of Wild Dogs. These Dogs are scary and they're big. Your spirit will know to put down tobacco. They say your soul knows, "If I put my tobacco down, maybe something will be good." Once the tobacco is down the Dogs become very playful and happy and the soul keeps travelling.

They say you will then travel to a spot where it leads to a gulley. It will be very dark down there. They say that you will have to make a fire to see light. So you make fire and follow a path to where it leads back up to blue skies again.

Once you are where blue skies are, you will see a river. Inside that river are the bones of many people that never made it across. They say that a great Serpent is living in that river, and that people are going to be very scared to cross it. On the other side of the river your ancestors and relatives who are already in the spirit world are there. And you will know that in order to get there where your relatives are, you will have to cross this river with the big Serpent in it.

So of course you will put down tobacco again, and when you do, the Serpent will turn into a log. You then cross the log to the other side and when you get to where your relatives are, you have a big feast with them.

And that's what I understand of the spirit world that Nenaboozhoo made for the Anishinaabe people. Now of course when you think about some of the religions of the world, it's pretty cool. It may be a little different than what other people believe, but that is a part of our people's beliefs.

Anishinaabe beliefs spread all over the Great Lakes, not just Serpent River. This was a common belief all over. People were always buried from East to West, with their feet facing West because they knew that's the way they had to travel. When they buried their enemies, they would face them the other way so they wouldn't have to deal with them in the afterlife. That is why when you go to old gravesites of the enemy they're buried one way or their bones are scattered all over, and when you go to an Anishinaabe grave they're buried East to West.

Jiibayaboos

Jiibayaboos is Nenaboozhoo's brother and was born from their mother Winona. He is half rabbit and half human. He was chosen to look after the path of the souls, otherwise known as the milky way.

Jiibayaboos

Mewzha, giiyaawag ezhkiniijig, nini miinwaa kwe, gaaniiwetaadjig. Epiichi chi-nchiiwag, ngoding gwa aapjii snagak bbong, mii giin nbod owi kwe.

Aapji gii wiisgendam owi ezkiniigid nini, gii-giizhendam wiindawaabmaadowi jichaagmaan. Aapjii gii-mesnan. aapji wii-wiiji yaawaan mii dash gii-maajiiendang wii dawaabamaad.

Gii gnoonaan kina gekaanh'an maa edonakiiwaad mii dash giiwiindmaagaasod, "Aabdek zhaawnong nikeying wii zhaayin, begish gda-semaam daanii bogdinad, miinwaa daa gwijimaadake, aapii-damkwad Jibiyaboos. Mii gwa daa mkwaad."

Gii-ndawaambjige, aa'aanj gwa, kina msiwe zhaawnong. Gegpii, gii-zaage'eshkan jiiskaan.

Shaweyiing jiiskaaning gii-waabmaan kiwenhzii'an. Kiwenhzii gii kida "Giispin biindgeyin maa jiiskaaning, daapkaanad Aki ge biindgeshkmaan".

Maaba shkiniigish gii miinaan kiwenhzi'an, Jibiyaboos, aanindmiingowewziwnan, mii dash gii biididet jiiskaaning. Gii-zaagam npaj'anake'iin jiiskaaning, mii dash gii maajii baa yaad jibeyi miikaanong.

Gii-gnaajiwan. Gaawiin gii nongoong gii-zhiinagsinoon oodi shpiiming, mii gwa dbishko Akiing.

Jiibayaboos

A long time ago, there was a young man and woman who were married. It was during a bad storm of an unusually hard winter, when she passed away.

Very upset, the young man decided he wanted to find her spirit. He missed her so much that he wanted to be with her and so he set off on a journey to find her.

He spoke to all of the elders in the village and they told him, "You have to travel South, putting your tobacco down and asking the earth where to find Jiibayaboos. You will find him."

This young man searched and searched and searched all over the South, and finally, he came to a lodge.

Beside the lodge, he saw an old man. The old man said. "If you come into this lodge, you're going to enter another world. At the end of the path, you'll find her."

The young man gave the old man, Jiibayaboos, some offerings and he entered the lodge. He went out the other side of the lodge and started travelling down the path of souls—the Milky Way.

It was beautiful. It didn't look like stars up there, it was like land.

Wa shkiniigish gii-shi-bimose ekwaamook miikaanhs.
Miijiigiziibi gii dgoshing. Aapii gii-waambdangiwe jiimaan.
Gii-bozgwashknii owi jiimaaning, mii gegwa gii niitkamkoswed
maa siibiing. Epiichi zhebwed, gii-maamnonnaambmad,
wiidgemaagnan, bmokzhiiwenid gewiin. Enso zhebwed, mii
gwa giiwin wiidgemagnan. Enso gnawaabmaad, mii sa go geye
gnawaabmigwad. Naasob-koswehwag tkaamkoswewad

Eshkam gii chi aangaashkaa. Ggii waabmag gwa shashgwagaa
maajajig, gaa shkitosjik, wijii-tkamiiwad. Kina dash wii gwa
binoojiinhyag gaa bmooshewejig gii-wenpanziwag wii-
tkamkoshwewad. Gaa gi banmagmigsewan dgowan. Kina
giitiyenh gii yaawag etkaamkoswegjik. Aanid gii skiitonaawaa
miinwa aanid gaawiin.

Wiiba gwa gii nii gwagshiwewag oodi ezhi gnaajihwang.

Wa shkiniigish gii-noondwann wayaa naam-
biingbiindeweshnoonid "bi giiwen" kida. Gii kwe
naaskowaan, gii aabtoojiinaan, minwa gii jiimaan mii
daash gii boozgwashnid wi jiimaaning wii skaabiid.
Gaagigenh bezhik gdo'owaan gii baamemigozin.

Gii yapiiska bskaabiid oodi kiweziinh jiiskaaning. Pii edgoshing
oodi Jibiyaboos gii kida "nishke? Mnoyaa."

Gii-chinendam owi shkiniigish mnoyaanid miinwaa gii
waabimaad, miinwa gii miigwechwendam kina gegoo
gaawaamdong oodi.

"Gaawiin mshi giin giitsesinoon. Ggiidoo gii bi-skaabi dash,"
kida Jiibayaboos

Gii ni maajaa owi shkiniigiish, gii ni zogaamoodi
baneyiingjiiskaan shkwaandeming, neyaap maanpii Akiing.
Mii dash maa gaani njii zogge'aajmotatwaadednakiijig
maaenjibaad, kina gaa waabdong miinwaa gaa gkendong.

The young man walked to the edge of the path and came to the edge of a river where he saw a canoe. He jumped into it and started paddling across the river. As he paddled, he noticed that his wife was paddling across too. Every time he took a paddle, she took a paddle. Every time he looked at her, she looked at him. They were in unison as they were going across that river.

The waves started to get big, and in those waves, you could see the bodies of those that tried to make it across but never made it. But all the young children that were paddling were going across the river with no difficulty. The waves wouldn't bother them. They turned and looked all around them, seeing a lot of people paddling across. Some made it and some didn't.

Pretty soon, they made it to the other side and it was beautiful.

The young man heard a voice coming from that water that said, "You have to go back home now." He ran up to her, held her, kissed her and then he jumped in the canoe to go back.

He made his way back to the old man's lodge. When he got there, Jiibayaboos said to him, "See? She's okay."

The young man was happy to know she was okay and that he had seen her, and grateful for all that he saw while he was there.

"It's not your time to go there yet. I called you to come back and you did," said Jiibayaboos.

The young man left and went out the other door of the lodge, back into this world. From there he went on to tell his story to the people of his village of all he had seen and learned.

Nenaboozhoo and the Great Flood of Lake Huron

Nenaboozhoo got mad at his grandmother, and broke the giant Beaver Dam at Baawating (Sault St. Marie). His grandmother got mad at him.

This created a Great Flood; which we now know as Lake Huron. This information has been passed down through the ages for thousands of years. In the chronicle of Nenaboozhoo this happened after what is known as his 'camping days' and after previous floods that took place.

Nenaboozhoo and Naadowe Ojiibik

This is the story of how the rattlesnake got the shaker at the end of its tail.

Long ago, there was a mom who was doing work in the village. She placed her baby in a tikinagan leaning up against the lodge poles inside her wigwam. As she was working, she noticed her baby was crying. She quickly went to tend to the baby and saw two bite marks on his leg. Apparently a snake had crawled into the wigwam and got startled when the baby started crying and bit the baby, but the mother didn't see it. The baby started to get sick and the mother went into a panic. She ran outside the lodge, crying for help, "A snake bit my

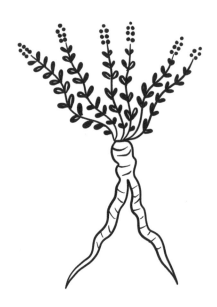

baby! A snake bit my baby! I need some help! I need some help!"

Nenaboozhoo was nearby and heard her cries, "I heard you crying for help and I came to see what's going on."

"A snake bit my baby. I need help for my baby!" she cried. She was frantic.

Nenaboozhoo took some roots out from his medicine pouch and he told the mom, "I want you to chew those roots and then put the chewed ball on the snake bite. Because you're breastfeeding, I want you to drink the tea made from these roots. The medicine will go through the breast-milk and it'll save the baby."

That's what she did. The baby got better as a result but the mother was still mad. She told Nenaboozhoo, "I want you to find that snake and kill it!"

Nenaboozhoo went off to look for the snake and found it but the snake was a smooth talker. He said, "I didn't mean to bite that baby; I just got startled when he started to cry."

"I know what I'm going to do," said Nenaboozhoo and he took wampum from around his neck that he was wearing as a necklace and he wrapped the snake's tail and told the snake, "From now on, when you get startled, I want you to shake your tail first. Don't be biting people. That way, it'll warn people to get out of the way."

That's how the rattlesnake got its tail.

Afterwards, Nenaboozhoo grabbed those roots he had in his medicine pouch and scattered them on the land. That is the origin story of the plant known as Naadowe Ojiibik, which is used among other things, to help cure snake bites.

Nmepin Gaa Zhi Waawiinhzod

Mewizha, yaa'aa gii yaa zhi zaagaganing, gichi nme, aapidji go gii mandido iidk wa nme, miidash giw anishinaaben pii takamkozhwewaat zhi zaagaganing, wa nme niw gaa zhi mowaat. Aapidji dash go giw anishinaabek gii gosaawaan niw gichi nimewon wii mizawe mowagoowaat, miidash gii maadjii giiwitaagaadesewaat zhi zaagaganing. Maaba dash Nenaboozhoo e inind, gii gikendaan e zhiwebadinik, miidash gii giizhiwendang wii gagwedji naadimawaat niw nninggonison, ji bowaa mowagoowaat niw gichi nimewon.

Mii sa ngoding, Nenaboozhoo gii ninokozhiwet naawonj aawoninik wi sa zaagagan, njida go gii nimbiigowewaagomige go, nando pogodjiwaat niw gichi nimewon. Wiiba sa go, mii wa gichi nme gii mookiit, mii go mizawe go wi jiimaan miinwaa niw Nenaboozhoon gaa zhigomaat. Aaniish, geyaabi dash go wa Nenaboozhoo gii bimaadizi, biindjina zhi nme masadaang.

Mii dash wa nme gegoo gonaa gaa zhimoozhendang, mii dash aanowi gagwedji zaagadji skwaanaat niw Nenaboozhoon.

Mii dash wa Nenaboozhoo wewiip gii takamaakosidoot doo jiimaanim zhi masadaaninit niw nmewan, mii dash gaawiin gii gashkitoosiin wa nme wii zagadji skwaanaat niw Nenaboozhoon. Mii dash wa Nenaboozhoo gii daapinang wi doo mookamaanim, gii maadjii podjiboowaat niw nimewon dehing.

How the Nmepin (Ginger) Got its Name

A long time ago, there was an extremely large Nme (Sturgeon fish) that would eat people as they paddled across the lake. People were very scared and often walked around that lake in fear of getting swallowed whole. Nenaboozhoo knew this and thought he would try to help his nephews from getting eaten.

So one day, he paddled out to the middle of the lake and started taunting the big Fish. Soon the big Nme came and swallowed him up with his canoe. Nenaboozhoo was alive in the Fish's belly.

The Fish was trying to spit him out because he knew something was wrong.

Nenaboozhoo quickly put the canoe sideways in the Fish's belly so the Nme couldn't spit him out. Then he grabbed his knife and started stabbing the Fish's heart.

Mii sa go gii nisaat niw giigoonhyan, mii dash gaashkwaa nsaat giw aanind nimewag wewiip gii maadjii nikozhewewaat jiigibiik nikeyaa, miidash gii maadjitaawaat mowaat wa nmepin e zhinikaanint, mii wi wii mashkowiiziinit niw dehe'waan, giishpin ginimaa naagach niw Nenaboozhoon mookiitaawigoowaat.

Miidash wa Nenaboozhoo gii gowaadaabaanaat niw gichi giigoonhan, gii wiishkosawaat niw, mii dash gimaapiich gii mowaat.

Gaabimisegin bboonan, niibna bemaadizidjik gii waabmaawaan niw nmewan mowaanit niw, wa sa nmepin. Gichi maamiikozhiwebaziwin gonaa aawon wi giishpin ooya zhi waambidjiget wi.

He killed that Fish and after he killed it the other sturgeons started to go onto the shoreline and started to eat the Nmepin to protect their hearts to make their hearts strong in case they were going to be attacked by Nenaboozhoo.

Nenaboozhoo dragged the big Fish onto the shore and smoked it and ate it.

Over the years many people have seen the Sturgeon eating the Nmepin. It's considered a blessing when you see that.

Nenaboozhoo miinwaa Ogaa

Mewzhaa, Nenaboozhoo gii bi midigoobiza, Anishinaabek aagonetomowaat maanda Biinojiinh Giiwaadziwin. Gaa gwa wiin gegoo maa baamziwin, geyaabi shko gii baanda aagognetaam. Aagonetadewak maamik niish ngwadodewadziiwaad. Moozook miinwa Aadikwag. Gii naadmowaan bezhik ngwadodewaadsiiwat aanwi gii gkendaan wii bwaa nbane naadmaged.

Moozook ntaa ndawenjigewag miinwa ntaa miigaaswag. Moozook gii nshkaadendmook Nenaboozhoo gaazhigiishendaang wii naadmowaad Aadikoogwag, aagonetaadewad, gii baa dawaabmaan wii nsot engaazit Nenaboozhoo. Niishtana eshoobiigaazjig, mii gaazoo ninwag gii noopnangoon. Gaawiin maanda nishizno, mii dash Nenaboozhoo gii zaagjishnaashkowind maa enjibot.

Nenaboozhoo gwa bangii kii niigaanii. Megwaatch gwa niizhwaak nsoonkewin, mii geskana gii nigaaset bmidjiwang. Gishpin bkobiigwaashkniyaanh, mii gwa wii nsigooyaanh maamik mii gaazoo ninwag shkweyaang ebiyaajig.

Ziibiising, giigoonh giibaamgwaangiinjin gii yaat, aa weh giigoohn gii gnawaabamaan Nenaboozhoon. Giigoonhyin gii goon "Giishpin naanaawgaam baamgwaangnon ka bigwaashkwon ma ngijibakwon miinwaa daash ka aanjigwaaskwon oodi nbaney yehn jiidgoshnon".

Nenaboozhoo and the Walleye

Years ago, Nenaboozhoo got involved with a tribal dispute over an adoption. It was not even any of his business, but he still took it upon himself to nosey his way into the dispute. Two families were arguing. One was the Elk family. And one was the Mooz (Moose) family. He took one family's side, even though he knew that it is never a good idea to take sides.

The Mooz Clan were known as very skilled hunters and warriors. The Mooz Clan became offended by Nenaboozhoo's decision to take the Elk Clan family's side in the dispute and set out to kill poor Nenaboozhoo. This was not a good thing and Nenaboozhoo was chased out of the village by twenty amazing painted warriors in pursuit behind him.

Nenaboozhoo was able to get a small lead on the warriors of about 200 arm lengths, when he got stopped dead in his tracks by a huge creek. He knew if he jumped in, he would be killed for sure, as the warriors were just behind him.

In the creek, there just happened to be a Fish floating where he was and the Fish was looking at Nenaboozhoo. The Fish said to him, "If I float in the middle, you can jump to me and step on my back and then take another jump to the other side."

Miidash go wewiib gii zhichiged. Mii dash miinwaa, Nenaboozhoo gii wiindamowaad giigoonhyan, "Nongwaa maadsek giizhgak ka bmiwdoonan gwenaanjwingin, e zaawaagin, mooksewnan gwiiwying onjii gii gzaadseyiin."

Giimooj ge'e gii aankesidoonan e gii naagin zhi bakwaanang. Mii dash mooz doodem miigaasooninwag daa gshkitoosiinawaa wii zhitchewaad wi naasaap miinwaa ji noop'nangod gaamziibiins.

Nenaboozhoo giibaap'aan niw biimnaashkaagwad, miinwa gii ngaamo doo maamiikwaandiiswin ngaamwin, ma megyaakwaag.

Gaawiika gii dimnewaasiiwaan Nenaboozhoon, gii giishendmoog sa gwa ngoding giidimnewanwaad maanda maamekwaandiwin, miinwa ga gegoo piitendizwin, kina ooya be baamsiwin be baamindaan. Mii sa gwa pane giigiiggowad, miinwa niibnaa nchiing giinoondaa naa waa pswewesnonik noogmowin noopming gbeyiing.

Mii gazhi dbebnong maaba Ogaa doo azowishing miinwaa doo giinko. Mii enji nendmowaad niibnaa, giiwednong eyaajig Moozoon Ododemwaan , miinwaa zhaawnoong eyaajig Odik Odemwaan, gii maamwizwag ngoding. Gaa shkwaa aagnetaadwat dash, mii majii swekaawaad, bemaadzijig, Moozok giiwednong giizhaawak miinwaa Adikwag zhaawnong gii zhaawak.

Nenaboozhoo agreed and did so very quickly. Nenaboozhoo then told the Fish, "From this day on, you will carry beautiful yellow spots on your body for your kindness."

He also sneakily added sharp spikes on its back, so the Mooz Clan warriors could not do the same thing and follow him across the creek.

Nenaboozhoo laughed at the warriors and took off singing his bragging song into the forest.

The warriors never caught up to Nenaboozhoo but vowed to get him one day for his bragging, rude and nosey behavior. Of course, they never caught him, and often his bragging song was heard echoing in the forest for years after.

This is how Walleye got its yellow spots and sharp spikes on its back. It's often thought that the Mooz people are the Cree and the Elk Clan people are the Ojibwe and they were one at one time, one tribe, but after that dispute the tribe split up and the Mooz people were said to have left heading Northwest, while the Elk Clan people started to go East.

Nenaboozhoo miinwaa Zaade Mtig

Ngoding gwa giimobiwe maaba Nenaboozhoo. Niibna zhaangenmigwad giiminoshkaagoon.Gaagwa giide zhisese, miigwa wiidimnigwod. Miisaa gaa zhi wabmaad mtigoon, gii gwejmaan wii gaazod.

"Enh, biinjgwoshkoni" kida mtig.

Miidash Nenaboozhoo gii biinjgwoshknid epiichi miptowaad emnashkaagojin. Gaawanh gii ji zhaabwii. Nenaboozho gii zogewe pii kina gaa jaakamgak, miinwaa kida.

"Gaa miin niin sa ka miigwechwe'in, miinwaa gegoo ka miinin, gii-gkaashyin."

Miigise kewewwin gii toon biinji mtigoong.

"Ngii gwiin-waamdaan odeh ji yaamon, ka miinnin daash bezhig" gii kida Nenaboozhoo.

"Miinwa ka-waawiinin 'Zaade' mtig ka zhinkaaz" gii kida.

Mii-dash maanda anoozwin 'Zaade' gaabi nji-baamgag.

Nenaboozhoo and the Poplar Tree

Nenaboozhoo was running from the enemy one time. There were many behind him. Time was running out and the enemy was going to catch him. Nenaboozhoo saw this tree and asked the tree if he could hide inside it.

"Yes, jump inside!" the tree said.

So Nenaboozhoo jumped inside and hid while the enemy ran by. He barely made his escape. When the enemy left and it was all clear, Nenaboozhoo jumped out of the tree and said,

"I'm going to thank you and reward you for hiding me."

He grabbed his eagle staff and placed it inside the tree.

"I'm going to give you a heart because I noticed you didn't have one" Nenaboozhoo said.

"And I'll also give you a name: Zaade," he added.

This is how the name and heart of the poplar tree came to be.

Pane aabdiseh Zaade mtig maa anishnabe bgosendmogosewin. Azoomanatig (Nswakomak) zhinkade nsawakosid owe mitig,waamdagosid mdimooyenh baabiiwat maa jiichaak miikaanang. Kidwag ngoding gwa pii nbo'ing gaa bmosemin ma oojiichaak miikanang gaa bi dgwaadamin maa nswakmok miikan. Nenaboozhoo gii ngadaan gshki e'owziwin zaade mtigoong, mtigook aankoobzowag nangong. Giishpin waamadaman zaade niibiishan bmaasing noodingong nangaaknenoon tibishko nangoonhsag.

Zaade mtig aabdisi aniishnabe bgosendmagosiwin teg, miinewaa nswakomwa miikan.

They use the poplar tree in ceremonies all the time. Azhoomanatig (Nswakomak) is the name of the crutch in the tree, which represents the split in the path where the old lady is waiting on the path of souls. They say that one day when we die, we will go along the spirit road and come to that Azoomanatig (Nswakomak). The tree is connected to the stars because of the power Nenaboozhoo left in the tree. When you look at the poplar leaves blowing in the wind, they twinkle like stars.

That is why we use the tree, and the crutch in the tree, in ceremonies.

E oonji pasaanhzawaat giw wiigwaasak

Mtigwak, ganoondiwok gwonda. Pane go ganoondiwok. Maanda dibaajmowin yaawaak dash dbaadjigaade, aanint mitigwak wi pii gii migiikaandiwaapan.

Maanda gii naadjimwabaniik giw anishinaabek, mewizha wa wiigwaas aatik, ngoding gii mimaamiikwaadjmatowaan wiiji mtigoon e zhi zhooshkonagayekozit. Kida sa "gwaabmim ezhigonaadjwiyaanh." Giyetin dash go aapiji go gii zhooshkonagayekozi wa miinwaa gaye aapiji go gii waabshkaandeni wi nagek.

Mii dash ngoding giizhigak, mii gaawaandagoon enaat wa wiigwaas, "nishke dash gegiin gdoo nagekom, aapiji go maanaadizi miinwaa nchiiwnaagozi. Gnawaabam dash geniin ndoo nagekom. Aapiji go zhooshkozi miinwaa ge'e aapiji go waabshkizi."

"Gaawiin nishizinoo wi ekidayin, gaawiin gonaa gdaa zhichigesii wi," gii kida sa wa gaawaandag, mii dash go wa wiigwaas geyaabi go epiichi aabiizmaat niw gaawaandagoon ezhimaanaadizinit doo nagekman.

Gaawiin dash gii gikenimaasiiwaan niw Nenaboozhoon gnawaabmigoowaat. Miidash gii patoot oodi yaanit niw wiigwaason maanda dash gii naan, "Aaniish enji madjiganoonat gaawaandag. Aapiji go maamiikoowaabiminaagoziwon miinwaa aapiji gonaadjwiwan doo nagekman maaba. Aapiji go gdoo madjizhiwebiz!"

Black Spots on the Birch Tree

The trees talk to each other. They talk to each other all the time. This is a story about when the trees got into an argument.

They say that many years ago the birch tree was bragging to the other trees about how smooth its bark was, saying, "Look at how beautiful I am!" The bark was in fact really smooth and pure white.

One day, the birch tree started to pick on the spruce tree, "Look at your skin. It's so rough and ugly. And look at mine! Smooth and white!"

"That's not nice, you shouldn't be like that!" responded the spruce tree while the birch tree just kept throwing rude remarks on how rough the spruce tree's bark was.

They didn't know that Nenaboozhoo was watching. He ran over and said to the birch tree, "Why are you being so mean to the spruce tree? Its bark is awesome and beautiful. You're so mean!"

Maanda dash gii zhi nkwetam wa wiigwaas, "Aaniish, nishke sa ezhi gonaadjwiyaanh!"

Mii dash wa Nenaboozhoo gii bookowaakobinaat bangii niw gaawaandagoon mii dash gii maadjiipashzhewaat niw wiigwaason, mii dash gii mazinset wa gaawaandag zhi wiigwaasi nagekong.

Mii sa wi nongom enji pasaanhzat wa wiigwaas, gaawiin dash go wiikaa miinwaa gii madjidoodawaasiin niw aanind mitigoon.

The birch tree's answer was, "Well, look at how beautiful I am!"

So Nenaboozhoo grabbed a spruce bow off the spruce tree and started whipping that birch tree, leaving little marks on it.

That's how the birch tree got the marks on it, and it was never mean to any other tree again.

Giigoonh Zhag'aay Aadzookaan

Nmaamnanendaan ndoo odenwesing bemaadzijig gii-
niigewag. Giigoonhyin, amikwan, miinwaa moozwan
gii-ndaadziwag. Nmakwendaan gii-waamdamaan
wiigwaamens gii-gaachiinyan. Aabta naamkamik gii-te
maanda wiigwaamens. Mtigo pakwaan gii-aawan. Aki gii-
te giji pakwaan wiigwaamensing. Kaa wiikaa zhaabgaasnoo
pakwaan. Biinji wiigwaamens, gii-te waasechigan. Gaawiin
gwa gwaasechigaanaa gii-zhinaagzinoo. Maanda waasechigan
gchi-bkaan gii-zhinaagot. Giigoonh zhag'aay gii-nji-zhichgaade.
Kiwenziinh ngii-kwejmaa gaadaat maa, "Aaniish gaa-zhi-
zhichigaadeg wedi waasechigan?"

Gii-kida, "Maziywayaan gii-aabidat."

"Wegnesh iw?" ngii gwejmaa.

"Giigoonh zhag'aay" gii-kida.

"Gmaamiikwaajim sa go" ndinaa, "aaniish gegoo
ezhaabiisnook enji-nakaasiwan?"

"Nooj maanda nishin pii dash ezhaabiisnook" gii-kida,
Nenaboozhoo maanda gii-miingoonaan. Aaniish ge nji-
aabjitoo'aamban waanak ezhaabiisnook maawnji-nishing
yaawmaan."

"Aaniish Nenaboozhoo gaa-zhi-biidmaagoying?" nda-zhi-
kwejmaa.

Fish Skin Window

I remember years ago in my village the people were still trappers. They lived on a diet mostly consisting of fish, beaver, and moose. During my childhood, I remember seeing a cabin. The cabin was half dug in the ground. The top of it was made of logs. On the top of the cabin, there was sod on the roof. The roof never leaked. Inside that cabin, there was a window. It wasn't just a regular window. This window was very, very different. It was made out of fish skin. So I asked the old man who lived there, "What is that window made out of?"

"Oh that's made out of Maziywayaan (burbot skin)," he said.

"What is that?" I asked.

He said, "That's a fish skin."

"Well that's very fascinating," I said, "how come you just don't use plastic?"

"I don't want to use plastic, this is even better" he said, "Nenaboozhoo gave us that. Why would I want to use grungy plastic when I can have the best of the best?"

So I asked, "How did Nenaboozhoo bring that to us?"

"Epiichi-miigaading maanda gii-zhiwebat" gii-kida. Ngodweyaangizid wiigwaamens gii-yaanaawaa jiiggaam. Gchi-sin gii-te baneyiing. Waa-miigaazjig gii-bi-njibaawag oodi zhaawnang wiikwed nikeying."

"Pane go gii-gotaanaawaa waabanong wiikwed nikeyiing" gii-ni-naajimo. Mii oodi gaa mi zhaawaad waa miigaazjig. Pane gii-kowaabwag ngodewaangizwaad gojiing wiya wii-bwaa-biidaaminaagozit. Ngoding ngodewaangizyaang ngii-yaamin, giji gchi sin shkweyaang wiigwaamensiing gchi-siniin ngii noondaamin gegoo nwewek wi sin."

Aabdek gii-oo-nda-gkendaanaawaa. Pane go gii-noondaanaawaan gegoo nwewemgak siniin ezhi-gkendamang gaa-bi-zheyaawaad Anishnaabek. Miinwaa pane go kina wiya noondaanaawaan gegoo nwewemgak megyaakwaak. Gii-oo-nda-gkendiigewag miinwaa. Pii gaa-ni-dgoshnowaad gidaabik, gii-dete'aakogewag.

"Wenesh maa eyaat? Gmina-aaw na maage gmji-aaw?"

Geskana gii-waamdaanaawaa zhiibaadnoos bibdek shaweying siniing, wiigasiinh mjimnidoons. Gii-ni-ngwaabminaagzi siniing. Gii-gkendmaawaan Nenaboozhoo aawnid biinji siniing. Mii ezhi-gshki'ewzid mshkoziiwinyaang noodinong.

Mii dash gii-kwedwewaad, "Nenaboozhoo gda-yaa na maa?"

Sa, gii ngwetwaan, "Enh, mampii ndiyaa. Giishpin bi-zhaayin mampii aabdek ka-miizh niibna miigwewinan." Gaa gegoo waa-miigwewaad. Gii-mnonendmook biinji siniing yaanid. Mii dash doowaach gii-bskaabiiwaad wiigwaamensing.

He said, "It happened a long time ago when they were fighting. There was a family that had a little cabin on the edge of the lake. And there was a big rock on the one side. The enemy would come up on through the South side of the bay."

He continued, "They were always scared of that South side of the bay because the enemy would go through there. The family were always checking outside that lodge to make sure nobody was coming. One time my family was there, and on that big rock behind the cabin, there were noises coming from that rock."

Naturally, the family went to investigate the noise. As we know, in the history of our people, hearing noises in a rock is very common, and everyone is always hearing noises from all over the place in the forest. So they went to investigate. When they got to the top of the rock they started to knock.

"Who's in there? Are you good, or are you bad?"

All of a sudden, they saw a little whirlwind come shooting up the side of the rock, a little dust devil. Then it disappeared into the rock. And they knew it was Nenaboozhoo inside of that rock because the wind is one of his powers.

So they asked, "Nenaboozhoo are you in there?"

Of course, he knocked back, "Yeah I'm in here. If you come in here you have to give me a lot of presents." Well they didn't have anything to give, but they felt good that he was inside of that rock so they went back to the cabin.

Aazho-dibikat gii-gchi-noodin. Gii-nchiiwat. Gii-maangaashkaa.
Miinwaa noondaanaawaa wiya dete'aakoget shkwaandeming.
Epiichi miigaading, gii-zegziwag, gii-nkwetaanaawaa dash
wii go shkwaandem. Maandaaginini maa gii bidakgaabwi
shkwaandeming. Gii-gkendmaawaan Nenaboozhoo aawnid.
Aabdek wii-biindganaawaat.

Gii kida, "ngii gnawaabminim, miinwaa ngi gkendaan kii
zegzim bmaadziyek. Gegoo nga-zhichige." Gii-ndoojiingedoo-
mashkimidaang, giigoonhyin gii-debinaan miinwaa aasmaatik
gii-pagnaan. Pii giigoonh ebagaskaakshing aasmaatik,
waasechigan gii bi aawan. Nenaboozhoo gii waamda'aan
bemaadzijig waa zhi nakaazwaad giigoonh zha'gaayan wii
waasechganwaad. Wii gkenmawaad wenesh waa bi dgoshing
shkwaandeming.

The next night, it started to get windy, it started to blow hard. There was a lot of wind. The white caps on that lake were just huge. Then they heard a knock at the door. Being war time, they were frightened, but they answered the door anyway. There was a very beautiful looking young man standing at the door. They knew it was Nenaboozhoo. So of course they invited him in.

He said, "I've been watching you guys and I know you've been living in fear. So I'm going to do something for you." And he reached into his packsack and grabbed a fish and threw it at the wall. When that fish hit the wall, it turned into that window. That's how Nenaboozhoo showed the people how to use fish skin for a window, so they could know who was coming to the door.

NAADIZIWIN KINOOMAAGEWIN

Maanda tibaadjimowin, owih ekwchigaadek ebi'miigaazod bi'zhaad shkowaandemin' gtibaaadjigaade. Anishinaabe debwetan pii bwang, owaa e'miigaanik gdaa bizhaamik gda wiigwaami shkowaandeming. Dash akinoomaagewin aawan epiichi ngogaaswod maage bigidenjigeng kaa wiika ooyaa e'aaw'wid gaan'bod wii nipiizod shkwaandemin, dash wiigowah zhiweying wiigwaamin nikeyaa dash. Debwejigaade jiijaakoog da gookeze shkwaandeming maage enji biindigeng miinwaa baabiiaawaan wiinwaa jiijaakman wa gaa nbwod epiichi biindigaajgaazod. Dash doodem gaa nbwod apane dash da daapnaa'aan wiinwaa e'zaagaa'waad weni zhiweying wii baamenjigaadesnok e'giibaadak maage emaanenjigejik jiijaakoog e'baabiijigejik. Nongo biinish wa giizhigak, piichin gaa gwaabndaawaa niibaabing, da nangaashkaawag shkwaandeming miinawaa nagam'mowinan da nagam'mok wii gwe zhaabwiichgaade naakinigewinan. Ndoo inendam gchi-piitendaagwod pane aabdek wii zhiitooyiing wiiwyiwaan dash kiinwi wi minidookewinkeng gaa bi zhichigewaad gda Gchi Anishinaabemnaa'nik gaa ni ngadmaagooyiing waa zhichgeying.

TRADITIONAL TEACHING

In the story, the 'threat of the enemy coming to door' is referred to. The Anishinaabek believe that also in death, your enemy may come to meet you at the door of your wigwam. So the teaching is that during burials or funerals you never take the body of someone who has passed on out through the door, but rather through the side of the building somehow. It is believed that the spirits attach themselves to the doorway or within the doorway and wait there to attach themselves to the spirit of the person who had passed as they are brought through the door. So, the family of the deceased would always take their loved one through the side to avoid bad or rival spirits that awaited them. To this day, sometimes you will see at traditional funerals, the procession will stop at the doorways and songs will be sung to try to preserve the protocols. I feel it's important that we always prepare the bodies ourselves so that the ceremony can be done the way our ancestors left it for us.

The Stranger with Big Ears

A long time ago, the Anishinaabek used to have a big wigwam that was set up from East to West. In the springtime they would go there and they would have a ceremony.

Over the years a lot of people would come there but one year something happened and they forgot to bring a drum inside the ceremony. After that everything began to go wrong and after a few years the people began to lose their way and grow very greedy.

One year, the leader who was a very big man and a very greedy man, was seated at the Eastern Door. He sat there with all kinds of moose fat and moose bones laying beside him and he didn't share any of his food with anybody. The greedy man at the Eastern Doorway was known to be mean. When he spoke, he always shook his fist.

The people had forgotten the ceremony and while they were in the lodge, they were just laying around, not even doing anything.

During this time when the ceremony was supposed to be happening, a man in the village got very sick. So his sister brought him to the lodge to see if she could get help for him there as that was what the lodge was supposed to be for.

She came into the lodge and explained to the people, "My brother is very sick. He's going to die."

The greedy man at the Eastern Door said, "Don't bother us here."

"What am I supposed to do?" she asked.

The greedy man said, "I don't know."

So she grabbed her brother by the arm, and carried him into the wigwam right into the middle. Her brother just curled up into a ball on the ground. He was going to die.

The sister looked around and said, "What's wrong with you people? How come you're not doing anything to help my brother? This is supposed to be a ceremony!"

"Get out of here!" The greedy man said.

Well, she got pretty mad, and she took off crying.

She started to run towards the lake. When she got nearby she saw a rock and climbed up on it. Just then she saw a nice big beautiful white birch tree and she thought to herself, "I'm going to get that birch bark, and once my brother dies I will wrap him up in the bark."

So that is what she did. She went to that tree and started to make a long cut downwards on the bark. This is what people used to do to get birch bark. They would get a long stick. At one end of that long stick, they split the end, and they jam a piece of flint in there so they could reach high up on the tree and begin to cut downwards. That is how they cut their bark. At that time of year, once you make that cut, the bark just wants to pop off.

As she was doing this, she looked on the ground, and she noticed something was staring at her. It was a little Bunny

Rabbit. It was just staring at her. She looked at the Rabbit, and said, "Can you help my brother?" That Rabbit just blinked at her, like rabbits do and hopped away.

Once she had finished cutting the bark off the tree she rolled it up and tied it up with a strand of willow bark. She carried the roll of birch on her shoulder and went back down to the wigwam where her dying brother lay.

She went back inside and placed the roll of birch bark beside her brother.

The greedy man at the Eastern Door didn't say anything, he just stared at her, while chewing on a piece of fat.

She looked at him and said, "You know what? You're a really mean man."

He didn't say anything, he just kept eating his fat and staring at her.

All of a sudden, the greedy man at the Eastern Doorway looked through the door, and he said, "Somebody's coming!"

Well, you know how Anishinaabek are, as soon as you say somebody's coming through the door, everybody's got to just stare! So they were all looking at the door and wondering who was about to come through the door.

Just then a man walked up. He was tall and he had two big eagle feathers sticking out from the back of his head. Those eagle feathers were immaculate. They were golden eagle feathers, the ones with the black tips. The ones that all the people want to have. He was very striking, this man. He was handsome and his clothing was beautiful and fully beaded. He had a certain thing about him that was very attractive.

He stood at that Eastern Door and the greedy man said, "Hold on stranger. You're not allowed in here."

The man replied, "You don't even know my power, you don't even know what I can do. For many years, your young people and your old people tried to shoot me with their arrows and I dodged every one of them. I was always fast and able to get away. Your arrows could never kill me."

The greedy man looked at him and said, "Before you enter this lodge, I want to see your power."

The man with the feathers looked at him, and smiled, "You have a bad attitude, don't push me."

So the greedy man walked up to him and pushed him.

The minute that he touched him, that man with the feathers jumped up high in the air and when he landed on the ground the whole ground shook and you could hear thunder way deep under ground. The man with the feathers looked at the greedy man and said, "That's my power."

Well, the greedy man at the Eastern Door at that point knew that the visitor was somebody very special. Everyone knew the man with two feathers was a holy man because he had a power that regular people didn't have.

So he was permitted to go in of course and as soon as he walked in, he said, "Why isn't anyone dancing for this sick person laying on the ground? How come all of you are just sitting there staring at him? How come nobody is dancing? Where are the drums?"

Nobody knew what to do. Of course, they just sat there with their heads down; they didn't even want to look at him. He said, "I command that you dance for this person that's on the ground. Dance for him, so that he can get well again." Still, nobody did anything. Maybe they were scared, or maybe they felt ashamed, no one knows for sure, but they didn't do anything.

All of a sudden, the greedy man at the Eastern Doorway said, "Look, somebody else is coming!"

Again, everybody looked at the door and a Wolf came walking in right into the middle and jumped over the man that lay dying on the ground. As he jumped a spark came flying from his tail in mid-air and spiraled down and went right into that dying man's mouth. As soon as that spark went into his mouth, the man stood up, and he was instantly cured.

The holy man motioned to the Wolf and said, "This is my brother, and his power is great. And because he cured this man, you must give him offerings. You have to give him something to eat for what he did. He will accept all of those bones that are laying on the floor. He will accept all that fat that is laying around." He said, "And he will accept all of that greedy man's food that he's got tucked away behind him."

So the Wolf started to eat up everything off the ground. And he cleaned up that big wigwam and he cleaned it up nice. All of the fat was taken off the ground and all of the wasteful food was cleaned up.

And of course, the little stash of food the greedy man kept behind him was gone too. At that point, everybody was the same. Nobody had more fat than anybody else. Nobody had more zaasganag than anybody else. Everybody had the same because everybody had nothing.

The holy man with the two feathers told the people, "I'm going to stay here, and I'm going to show you how to do this ceremony again. You were told once, and you forgot, and I'm going to show you one more time."

He stayed for a while and he taught them and drew everything for them in the sand. He drew the ceremony and told people where they were to sit. The women on this side, the men on that side, the fire here, the drum there – everything was explained to them. Then he said, "Just to make sure that you remember, I'm going to draw this for you on birch."

The Wolf came up to him with the moose bone, and plopped it in his hand. With that moose bone, he went to that birch bark that was going to be used to wrap up that dying man, and he drew everything into the birch bark with the moose bone. The birch that was going to wrap up the dying man now had beautiful pictures of the ceremony on it with instructions of how it was supposed to be conducted. Even the songs were drawn on there. This birch bark, they say, had a heartbeat when people held it; it was alive.

The man with two feathers walked over to the greedy man at the Eastern Doorway, and gave it to him. He said, "This is to remind you of what goes on in here. As a reminder, my brother the Wolf is going to stay and live with you. He's going to live outside that Eastern Doorway so that people will not bring the sickness of greed or those bad ways inside here anymore. He's going to protect this lodge. All he requires for his offerings is fat and bones."

After he was done he told the people, "It is my time to go, my journey continues."

The people pleaded with him, saying, "Don't go! Don't go! Stay!"

"I can't stay, I have to go," he said, "I'm going West."

So, as he walked towards that Western Door, people started to sing for him. They were so happy he came, because he changed everything for them. He gave them life again and he gave them hope.

The drum was sounding strong again as he walked out that Western Doorway, people crowded up around the door just to see him go.

They watched as the holy man walked down the hill to a little gully. And when he walked back up the hill he wasn't a man, he was a Rabbit. He was a little Bunny Rabbit hopping up that hill.

And so that's how they saw that Waabooz walking towards the sunset. To commemorate what that holy man did for them, to commemorate everything that he showed them, they drew his picture on the rock where the Rabbit was first seen. They grabbed the sacred paint, the Onaman, and they painted him smoking a pipe, with his big ears, or feathers, to commemorate what he had done for the people.

Burial Sites

In the Spanish Residential School, there was a young boy that died of chicken pox. They say he had lumps on his face and he passed away. So in Serpent River his family and the people of the village took that small child and wrapped him in birch bark and they buried him at the old village site. There is a big graveyard in the old village site. The people wrapped him up in birch bark and placed him in a shallow grave.

But the people who ran the Spanish Residential School claimed, "No, because he was baptized, we have full rights to that body, under god's authority."

The people from the school actually went to the Indian burial site in Serpent River and they dug up the boy from his grave and they took his body back to Spanish and put him in an unmarked grave. That is where his remains are still today.

That the people from the Spanish Residential School stole the body from the grave and put the body in another grave is not unique or strange, because they probably did that all the time. What makes this story unique is they actually documented everything that happened with the family, and with the burial, with everything.

The French person documented what he saw and wrote, "When we arrived at the graveside the Anishinabe were dancing at the grave…they said they were celebrating the life of the young person, and that they were dancing in circles around the grave."

They recorded that on the grave, on top, the Anishinaabek had made a little wigwam made out of birch bark and inside that wigwam they had placed food. On the West side of the grave they had a fire, and they said that they were cooking on the fire. The ritual of dancing around the grave would last for ten to fifteen minutes and then stop. The people would eat, tell stories then the dancing would start again.

So, when the Residential School people went up to this grave and said, "We have to take this body," the Anishinaabek said. "You can't bother the body because it's travelling, it's going West, it's going home." That's what he recorded them saying.

The Residential School people said, "We have no choice," and the Anishinaabek said, "If you bother it, maybe Nenaboozhoo will get mad at you."

Of course the French people from the Residential School laughed, because they felt like they were the boss of everything and I guess, and at that time, they probably really were.

The Residential School people started to dig the grave, and again they recorded everything, and what they said was that when they started to dig the grave, which is located uphill a little bit from the lake, the mother was crying down at the edge of lake. The Anishinaabek said that the Residential School people couldn't understand why she was crying so hard because her son was going to go to heaven and not hell.

They took the body of her son and they unrolled the birch bark, and what they found inside the birch bark were supplies. They found dried meat, they found dried berries, they found a little knife, they found a candle, they found a little axe, and moccasins and the boy was painted red with Onaman.

The Residential School people wanted to 'clean' the boy up, so they actually took the body back to Spanish and they washed the sacred paint off the boy and put him in a suit of some sort, and they buried him in an unmarked grave, and never told the parents where he was buried.

When you listen to that story, it's a very tragic story right? The tragedy is not just the fact that the boy was stolen from our gravesite, but our way of life, how we looked at the spirit world, was also stolen too. Because all those little children buried at the Residential School, obviously their family believed that there was a spirit road that went from East to West and all of our customs and ceremonies we believe in were robbed from them when their children were taken and buried in unmarked graves.

Nenaboozhoo nganaan Anishinaaben

Memdige akina gegoo e'aabjikaasying nongo gii miingonaa Nenaboozhoo.

Wiinwaa kidok aanind gaa bi'maadiziwingin, Anishinaabe gii maajtaa naagdood miikan bkaan nikeyaa, gii maajii naagdoonaawaa bkaan miikaanhs. Nenaboozhoo gii maanaastam miinwaa gii wiindamowaan bemaadzinjin, "zaam kiinwaa gda nizhaam bepkaan miikaanhs, niin bkaan wii nizhaa. Aabdek nwii ni'maajaa. Zaam kina gegoo gaa miin naa, ngii maanaastam miinwaa aabdek nwii maajaa." Mii dash Nenaboozhoo gii ni maajaat.

Niin apane gii noondaan wa Nenaboozhoo, gii maajaa zaam e'waabshkii'ejik bemaadzijik gaawiin bshigendmaasiiwaan, gii noondaan zaam Anishinaabe gii ngshki'aawaan, gii wnendamaawaan miinwaa da aadziwinim. Gii ni'maajaa miinwaa gii ni'zhaa biinji siniing yaa dash o-Nookmisan. Aanind bemaadzijik kidok nooj geyaabi Giiwednong yaa; aanind kidok waasa nikeyaa Epingishmak, aanind bemaadzijik kidok Waabnong nikeyaa. Ngii noondaan Dibaadjimowinan kina goji.

Nenaboozhoo Leaves the Anishinaabek

Virtually everything we use today was given to us by Nenaboozhoo.

They say that quite a few generations ago, the Anishinaabek started to go the wrong way, they started to go down the wrong path. Nenaboozhoo got offended and he told the people, "Because you're going down the wrong path, I'm going somewhere else, I have to leave. Because after everything I gave you, you offended me and I have to go." So Nenaboozhoo left.

I always heard that Nenaboozhoo left because the white people didn't like him, but I also heard it's because the Anishinaabek offended him because they forgot about him and his ways. He left and he went into a rock and is there with his grandmother. Some people say it's further North where he is, others say it's far in the West, some people say it's in the East. I've heard stories of all those places.

Ten Men Fasting - Mkadekewag Mdaaswi Niniwak

Mewzha, mdaaswi niniwag gii-ni-maajaawagwii-oomkade-kewaadwaanhzhing. Wii-goji gkendmowaad aapiish Nenaboozhoo eyaad.

Nenaboozhoo gii-ni-majaa, zaam Anishnaabek gaay gii-mnadenziinaawaan kina miingoweswinan gaa-ngadmaawdwad, miinwa bkaan gegoo gii-naagdonaawaa miidas giimaajiinaagdoowad owi shki shoyaawin.

Gii zhaabwaabwog gii bwaajgewaad maabak mdaaswi jiiskiwniniwag gii gkendaanaawaa aapish Nenaboozhoo endaanid. Giigkendaanaawaa ngoji Waanang nikeyaayaat. Niizhgon onjiBaawating. Niizgon gii bmosewok. Pii nidgosnaawaad oodi waanzhing, gii nsaakshka iyowaanzh mii maa Nenaboozhoo gii yaad. "Waagnesh waa-yaa-mek?" gii shigwede.

"Ndo gweji mkaanaanon gkendaaswin ji bskaabi debnamonggaa bi zhewebak mewzhaa." Nenaboozhoo gi-wiikmaan wii-biindigenid.

Ten Men Fasting – When Nenaboozhoo Left

A long time ago, ten medicine men set out to go fast in caves. They wanted to seek visions to try to find out where Nenaboozhoo was.

Nenaboozhoo had left because he felt that the Anishinaabek were not honouring all of the gifts that were left to them and that they started to follow a new way.

As a result their visions, the ten medicine men were able to know where Nenaboozhoo lived. They knew he was somewhere in the East, a two-day travel from Baawating. So they walked for two days. They arrived at a cave, and when they got there, the cave opened up. Nenaboozhoo was inside and said, "What would you like?"

"We're trying to find knowledge so we can get back to the way things were before," the medicine men replied. Nenaboozhoo invited them in.

Giiw mdaaswi naandwejiiwniniwak gii
biingaadewsewagwaanhzhing, miish gwa wewiip,
beshig owi gii-gweddedmshkiki wa naadmaagwad wii-
gogge bemaadsid. Nenaboozhoo gii-
miinaan ngo mshkimod jiikenhnsan, giinaan wii-
miijidnwi jiibkenhnsan. Wewiip gaashkwaa mijiidnwi jiibkenhsan, mkaade asin gii-bi-
-owi, mtakamik giibongiishin.

"Nbe, gaagge-bemaadziwin gga-yaan."

Gaag gwa gegoo ndwaaj gii-kidsiiwag gii aanind niniwag.

"Aanish maanpii enji yaayeg?" "Aanish gaa bin-jii-shaayeg?"
Nenaboozhoo gii-shigwede.

"Gdaand-wendmigoo wii-bi-bskaabiyin," gii kidwag.

"Gaawiin nwii pskabiisiin, gaawiin gdo giizhiitaasiim. Gonimaa
nga bskaabii baamaa, nango dash gwa, maajiinikndaanis.
Ka kiinoomaagwaa enaabdakin mskikiin. Ge dash wiigwa ga
baamendmaasiiwaa. Pii wii dawaabmaadwiidgemaagnan da
mkowaanwiin gwa."

Gwi mdaaswi naandwejigeniniwok gii
ngadaanawaaowiwaanzh, gii ni-skaabiwag.

Enibskabiiwaad, eni piiskaawaad, bezhig ow nini gii nsaa-
waabmaan nwiw Nenaboozhoo odaansan.

Pii kina ekshkozowaad ekizhebaawgak, gaa-maajaagobane
iidik. Gii nda waabamaawaan, miish gwa eta go gaa
waabamaawaad bineshiinhan tikoning mnadbinid, gii
gkenmaawaad wiin aawanid, gii gzike dash.

The ten medicine men walked into the cave, and right away, one of them asked for medicine that would help him live forever. Nenaboozhoo gave him a bag of roots and told him to eat the roots. As soon as the man ate, he turned into a black stone and fell on the ground.

Nenaboozhoo said, "There, now you'll live forever."

The other men didn't dare say anything.

"Why are you here? Why did you come?" Nenaboozhoo asked

"We want you to come back," they said.

"I'm not going to go back. You're not ready. I may go back later; for now, take my daughter with you. She will teach you all about the medicines. But you can't bother her. When she wants to find a husband, she'll find a husband on her own."

The ten medicine men left the cave and started travelling back.

On their way back, one of the men looked at the daughter the wrong way.

When they all woke up in the morning and looked for her they saw a Bird sitting on a branch and they knew it was her and she flew away.

Gaawiin wiikaa dash gii mkoziinaawaa gkendaaswin gaa-ndwaamdamwaad.

Ka gkendaanaan Nenaboozhoo ge'e geyaabi wiijii waasiin bemaadzinid. Maanda aabji snagag, snaghendming wnishnang, da ni teni gdi binoonhjiinhagmin wii yaamawaad ebiinaagmigmaage gnmaage baanak nesewin wii teg.

Gda yaamin megwaa enishiwebak bnaajchigaadek kina gegoo maanpii gda kiimnaan. Maanpii Naadwegamiing temgadoon mji'iiwish an engogaadegin, niigan naabwin ge'e ki gkendasiinaan waa ni zhiwebak. Aanwichgeniniwag gii biidaade gwa maanda gete Anishinaabek maanda gda kiiminaan. Zaazhi gwa miinwaa gii-gkendaanaawaa giizhaa waa ni zhiwebak. Kina kii-noondaanaan ninda dbaadjimoonan. Ngii noondam gegwa, megwaa gegoo wii-zhiwebak maanpii akiing. Mii gwa eta nishinaabe ge zhaabwiid maamii weweni ge naagdood wi mskwaa miikaan.

Giishpin wiika gegoo etegwen wii gaa giismang maaba Nenaboozhoo wii naadmaagoyiing mii sa nongo. Nenaboozhoo aawi egimaakdang bmaadziwin. Gaawiin nsatamoomgasnoo ji wiindmaagengban. Kii dowaabmaanaan pane gchi mshkiki gaa gkendang. Aaniish gaa nji boontaaying?

Mdaaswi niniwag da mkadekewag epiichi miigaading. Mii ezhi bgosendmang Nenaboozhoo da bi bskaabiid. Nenaboozhoo gii kida pii abjigwa dawendmang da biyaad mii maanda, nbaabii'aa.

They never found the information they were looking for.

We know that Nenaboozhoo is not with the people anymore. So I started to think that in such a dire time when we are so confused and so lost, and a time when we don't know if the future generations will have clean water or clean air to breathe.

We are in a time when the nuclear industry has destroyed so much in our homelands. We have one of the largest nuclear waste sites in the world, it's right on the edge of the great lake Huron. So our future is uncertain, we don't know what's going to happen. Some of the older prophets, the old people say that some disaster is going to happen and only the Anishinaabek are going to survive, we all heard those stories. And I've heard that during this time that when something is going to happen to this earth that the Anishinaabek will survive, the ones that choose the way of the wigwam of course will survive.

And I often thought that if there was ever time that we need to petition Nenaboozhoo to help us it would be now. Nenaboozhoo is the one that is the master of all life, it doesn't make sense to not at least throw it out there. We used to search for him before, we used to look to him for that grand medicine before, but not now, now we tell the stories. But maybe it's time we look for him. Why wouldn't we?

They say in the future that ten men will go fasting during a time of great war and it's in our hopes that Nenaboozhoo will return. Nenaboozhoo said when we really really need him, he'll come back. I believe that. I am waiting.

Nenaboozhoo miinwaa Anishinaabe Kendaasowin

Kiinwi kii miindgomi chi miigwewinan gaa bi'migweyeng maadiziwining biinish maadiziwining. Kiinwi gda tibaadtaa'naa wiigwaam, wiigwaas jiimaan, gchi twaa miigsaabiigan, animosh midaabaanes, miinwaa gda tibaadta'naa akina nenda Nenaboozhoo gaa miindagoying, dash aaniidash kiinwi enji aabijibkaasiisiiing nenda noongo? Niin nda nendam jida eta enji nakaasiiwang wi gdoo ngadendaanaa wi nikeyaa maadiziwin eyaamin nongo.

Akina etek gikendaasowin akina Akiing, wiinwaa kidok naasaap: wi zaam niibna gda aabjikaasnaa miinwaa gda daapnaa'naa zaam niibna gegoo. Nda nendam Nenaboozhoo geyaabi daa'aan niibna waa miinaajin Nishnaaben. Nda nendam tibaadjimowiniwaan gek'aanjik, gchi piitendaagodoon, ekdoomgakin geye. Gaawiin eta tibaadjimowinan, nmishomis-ko gii kida, "Ngii zhigaadese ko Elliot Zaagi'iganiing, Ngii zhaami ko Nagek Zaagi'iganng. Ngii mokzhowemi jiimaaning. Gdaa zhichige wi."

Enh, aambe zhichige'daa wi. Mii e'kidowaad Gek'aanjik. Kiinwin aabdek kwii zhichigemi e'kidowaad.

98

Nenaboozhoo and Anishinaabe Education

We were given such precious gifts that were passed down from generation to generation. We talk about the wigwam, the birch back canoe, the sacred wampum, the dog sled, and we are talking about all these things Nenaboozhoo gave us, how come we don't use them now? I think that the only reason we don't is that we are accustomed to the lifestyle we have now.

In every discipline of science all over the world, they are saying the same thing: that we are just using too much and taking too much. I think that Nenaboozhoo still has a lot to offer to our people. I think that the stories of our elders, they're very important, they hold a lot of meaning. Not just the stories, but my grandpa used to say, "I used to walk to Elliot Lake, I use to go to Bark Lake. We used to travel there by canoe. You should do that."

Yes, let's do that. It's what the Elders say. We have to do what they say.

Gii yaa enji maawnjidiwaad waasnaago miinwaa gii tibaadtaanaa'aa kinomaagewin miinwaa wa zhi zhichigaadek Anishinaabe akinoomaagewin miinwaa waa zhi kinomaageng.

Gii aawan e'znagak gaa nji giigdowaad, ngii gnwiinwinendam, gaawiin ngii nsastaawaasiig wi gaa kidowaad zaam gii znagendaagwod. Kidowinan zaam gnoosnoon, miinwaa ngii wnishin. Gaawiin gii dgoshnisii zhe'e wii nokiiyaan en'dwendaagwag miinwaa ngii maanaajzhayaa zaam wiinwaa miigaadwag. "Gda giigid na? Gda kid na gegoo?" gegpii, gii kidwag.

Ngii kid, "Gaawiin niin da nsastasiin mziniganan maage kina ezhi kidooyek kidwinan zaam eyaamaa eta akinoomaagswin naanan kendaaswin dash gaawiin gnabaach ndaa kendasiin, dash nda nendam memoonji shpaak nikeyaa kendaaswin kiinwi wa gdaa miinaanaanik e'shkiniigjik maampii akiing. Miinwaa mooshkin gwa eta nishnaabemong. Nda nendam mii wi memoonji shpaak kinoomaagewin gdaa miinaanaanik gwiiji Nishinaabenaanik. Miinwaa menji shpaak kendaaswin owah miinaaying gda bemaadizijik."

Gaawiin ngii gkendasiin memoonji mshkoo'ziimigak wi etek nda nendamowining maage ndeh'iing. Miinwaa nda nendam Nenaboozhoo kii miingonaa naakinegewin. Nda nendam Nenaboohoo kii miingonaa miikan naakinegewin waa zhi bmaadiziying. Akina gii maakbiigaade niw tibaadjimowinan. Nda nendam kiinwin aabdek kwii kendaa'naa, miinwaa nda nendam wii biidooying wi wii maadzim'migak miinwaa gijitoo'daa miinwaa zhaadaa neyaab mtigowaakiing. Nda nendam goji eyaad wa waaboos, wa mzinbii'igan zhi gnabaach nga zhaa maa miinwaa nga'saa semaa zhi miinwaa nga kwedwe gegoo.

I was at a meeting the other day and they talk about education and how to make an Anishinaabe education and curriculum. It was a very complicated meeting, like my mind was puzzled; I couldn't understand what they were saying because it was too complicated. You know the words were too big, and I was lost. I couldn't just get in there to do the work that was needed and I felt bad because they were fighting. Finally, they said, "Can you speak? Can you say something?"

I said, "Well I don't understand the papers or all the lingo because all I have is a grade five education so I can't possibly know, but I think the highest form of education we can give our young people is on the land, and completely 100 percent immersed in the language. I think that's the highest form of education we can give our people."

I don't know what's stronger than that in my mind and in my heart. And I think that Nenaboozhoo gave us the blueprint. I think that Nenaboozhoo gave us the road map to how to live. Everything is coded in those stories. I think we need to know, and I think we need to bring that to life and take a risk and venture back into our forests again. I think the place where there is a Rabbit, the pictograph there, maybe I'll go there and put some tobacco there and ask a question.

Kid'daa Nenaboozhoo eyaa zhi biinji, waanzh, miinwaa
giishpin nwii kwedweyaanh gegoo, gaawiin nga kwedwesii
wii maadziiyaanh pane. Gnabaach ndaa kwedwe, "Aaniish wa
zhichigeying kiinwi aawying Anishinaabe bemaadzijik? Aaniish
Anishinaabe waa zhichiged aanji gyakwaadziying neyaap ji
bskaabiyiing gaa bi zhi bmaadziwaad Nishinaabek? Maage,
waa zhi zhaabshkamang waa ni zhiwebak?"

Nwii kwede gchi-kwedjimowin. Niibna bemaadzijik gaawiin
gikendasiinaawaa e'zhiwebag maage wegnesh niigaan waa
ni zhiwebag. Nda nendam tenoon gegoo oodi wa miingoyiing
niw nkwetmownan miinwaa aabdek Nenaboozhoo da aawi
bezhig.

Let's say Nenaboozhoo is in there, in that cave, and if I was going to ask a question, I won't ask to live forever, I would probably ask, "What can we do as an Anishinaabe people? How can Anishinaabek do the things right again, to get back to how we were? Or how would we survive in the future?"

I'll ask a question like that because you know what, those are big questions. And a lot of people don't know what's happening or what the future will hold. But again I think that there are things out there that can give us those answers and of course Nenaboozhoo would be one of them.

OTHER ORIGIN STORIES:

How Chipmunk got its Stripes: The Origin of Sickness and Cures

The Anishinaabek have always learned from the Animals and four Sacred Winds. The Animals were always held in high regard for their knowledge and sacred walk of life. The Anishinaabek were so connected to the four-legged, and to the ones that swim and crawl, that they could communicate and shape-shift into each other. The Animals can still shape-shift into the Anishinaabek to this day because they never lost their respect for all of creation.

This natural balance between man and animal is needed for all of creation to survive. There have been many times in the past where this balance has been tested and broken unlawfully by the Anishinaabek. The Elders say there was harmony amongst all of creation.

The Six Spirits: Wabano, Zhowanong, Eshpingmok, Giywaydinong, Giizhik and Aki requested this balance when Nenaboozhoo created the earth. These spirits are a force that is in everything. There is no escaping their awesome power and great mystery. They are the natural laws that surround us, and once the two-legged decided to be bigger than them, great sickness was cast upon the earth.

Here is a story that explains the origin of how sickness came to be.

Once the Anishinaabek decided to be rude and wasteful. They over-harvested the animals and began walking over their food. Bones of the Animals were scattered everywhere and often covered pathways and trails.

The Animals were very scared of them and decided to meet about the disrespect for all living things that was being displayed on the trails.

In this meeting it was decided to send a delegate to the Anishinaabek to confide their issues to them in hopes of some sort of resolution.

This delegate, who was a Brown Bear, was killed right away as it walked into the village and the corpse was left to rot on a hillside.

The Animals were furious and held another council meeting to decide what to do.

The Chief of the Bears stood up (who was a Great White Bear) and spoke and said, "We must kill the two-legged or there will be no more four-legged left. They have shown great disrespect to us, despite us giving them our sacred medicine: our flesh. My Nation is strong and we will destroy them."

The Great White Bear then gathered his Nation together and they had a sacred council meeting. It was agreed that one Bear would give his life and the other Bears would make bow strings out of the skin around his neck and charge the two-legged head on with a great vengeance.

They made the bows and arrows but ran into difficulty. Their hands and feet could not pull the string back on the bows that well. Their arms and legs could only bend so much and didn't have the flexibility needed to shoot the bow and arrow with any sort of accuracy.

The plan was good, but not good enough to carry out the mission.

Again all of the Animals decided to gather in great council to discuss how to destroy the wicked two-legged. After long deliberation, it was decided that there was only one way to kill them: to curse them using their strongest medicine. Each animal provided a curse against the two-legged.

The Deer had a curse that would cripple the two-legged at the knees.

The Wolf had a curse that would hit them in the back of the legs causing cramping and sometimes nausea.

The Owl had a curse so powerful it dropped the two-legged down to the ground and killed them instantly.

The Fish cursed them with skin ailments and bad weather, many two-legged would drown mysteriously due to the Fish's curse.

They would also make people dream of snakes and such, causing them to lose their appetite and die.

The Spiders would spin webs in the Anishinaabek brains causing them to go insane and to kill themselves.

The Birds sang songs and would fan the sickness down on people with their wings.

It was a massive attack with brutal consequences for the Anishinaabek. But what else could be done? The Anishinaabek had over-populated and began destroying the earth.

The attack on the two-legged worked and they began to perish and suffer at an amazing rate. No Anishinaabe was immune to this war the Animals had waged against them, and they were thinned out in numbers almost to the point of extinction. It was agreed by the Animals to completely wipe the two-legged off the earth for their absolute disrespect for all of living creation.

The Anishinaabek didn't know where the sickness was coming from and created big fires to burn and kill the sickness. The people started to cut themselves to release the sickness, but it was too great. The sickness that was caused was too strong.

Chipmunk attended the council meetings of the Animals and knew of what was said and knew the strategies. He also knew which animal's curse caused which symptoms and which ones were the deadliest. Chipmunk knew that the four-legged were not going to stop their mission and decided to intervene at the risk of losing his life.

He went on a warrior's mission. He decided to go and tell the Anishinaabek of what was happening and when he told them the Anishinaabek decided to hold a sacred council.

The Anishinaabek knew that their wicked ways had caused the sickness, and agreed to be good-hearted people again, like their grandparents were.

It was decided to give offerings of tobacco to the plants and ask them to provide cures for the sickness that was spread upon the earth. The plants agreed because they wanted the fires to stop burning and because they had a compassion that was unmatched in the natural world. They agreed to fight back the curses with their medicine and it started working with every offering of tobacco that was given.

For every sickness, there was a cure by the plants. Life was restored for the people in an instant.

The plants also told the Anishinaabek that they had seen the sickness roaming the forests and that it would perish in the fires that were created. They instructed the Anishinaabek that if a person offends the animal before or after taking its life, to make a small fire on the trail on their way home and to lay tobacco and beg for forgiveness. This was to kill the curse that the animal would send to them after they lost their life. The curse would follow them on their trail and go into the fire and die. If this fire was not made as instructed, it would be possible the curse would go into the village and strike upon the closest person.

The plants also told the Anishinaabek that this type of curse would be in effect until the Animals were satisfied with the amount of respect and dignity that was given.

The Animals found out that Chipmunk told on them because the Owl was listening with his big ears. When he told the Anishinaabek of what was happening, the Animals got very mad and chased Chipmunk under a pile of brush, scratching him on his back with their claws. This is why Chipmunk has those lines on his back today.

It was agreed in the council by the Anishinaabek never to kill the Chipmunk for the great heroic deed that he did to save the people. This is also the origin of sickness and the mighty cures that are found in the sacred green blanket that gives us life.

Today when we are met with sickness, it is understood that we are under attack from a force that is often greater than us, and we still turn to the natural world for help. The natural world is only a reflection of the spirit world.

To prevent sickness we should never be greedy, wasteful or boastful of our hunting. When we brag about how good of a hunter we are, or waste the hide or head, we are only inviting sickness into our village. When we don't brain tan the hide of the moose or deer, we are just asking for trouble. The moose has such a big life and when it gives its life, it gives all of it. We need to use all of it.

We have somehow programmed our brain into believing this is superstition and not real. We have tricked ourselves into not believing in natural law that governs everything. We are quickly shape shifting into the greedy wasteful people that are depicted in this story.

I make a plea to our good-hearted people to teach the next generation about such things, so our people can survive. Elders say time is running out.

Gaa-binjigaadek Jiizikaan

Gii-gdagendam nini zaam daansan gchi-aakoziwan. Gwiinwi-zhichiged mii gii-zhitood wiigwaam wii-minoyaanid daansan miinwaa wii-naandwi'aad mnik go naa gewiin gegkendang, eshkam go ni-aakozid. Gii-giizhendam wii-mkadeked, wii-bwaajged waa-zhi-naandwi'aad daansan.

Gaa gegoo gii-bwaadziin, gii-giizhendam wii-zhiitaa'aad daansan pii nbonid. Gii-nendam wi wii-zhitmowaad e-ginaajiwang gwiiwnan wiin da shwaach miiyaang nikeyaa Epingishmok.

Gii-zhitoon mtigo-dsoonaagan. Gii-toon bmide sabaabiing wa dash wesiinh zhaazhaangdang wi sabaab gii-binjibaa wa mtig mii dash gii-aabzikoozod wa wesiinh. Pii maanda gii-zhichigeng, wii-daapnaan pkindaagan wii-zhitwaad genaajwang waa-biiskamnid shkwaa-bmaadzinid. Gaa go gbeying gii-zhidtaasii wii-nsonaajin jiigwan.

E-ni-naaskowaad, gii-gnoongoon. Gii-sgisdeshkoza eta.

Jiigwan gii-goon, "Aasnaa bgidjwebnishin nbimnaawas miinwaa nda-baabiigowok biidoowaanh miijim."

Wa nini gii-kida, "Ndaanis gchi-aakozi miinwaa nda-gijitoon wii-zhimaa'aag genaajwang waa-biiskang shkwaa-bmaadzing. Geyaabi dash gdoo-bmaadis, ka-bgijwebnin."

The Origin of the Shaking Tent (Jiizikaan)

There was a man who was in despair because his daughter was dying from a mysterious illness. All he could do was make the wigwam comfortable for her and try to remedy her with the knowledge that he knew. As her illness progressed, he decided to go fast for the medicine to save his daughter's life.

He did not receive a vision for what he was looking for and decided to prepare for his daughter's death. He thought that he would like to make her a real nice set of clothes for her final travel to the West.

He made a trap with wood and a heavy deadfall. He placed fat on the string that was holding the tension to the pin that was holding the weight of the tree. Once the animal chewed the string, the dead fall would come crashing down and kill the animal. Once this was done, he was going to take the fur and make his daughter something nice to wear for the afterlife. He quickly caught an animal in his trap. It was a Fisher.

When he approached the Fisher, it began to speak to the man, as it was only trapped on the toe.

Fisher told the man, "Please let me go. I have small children to feed and they are waiting for me to bring back food for them."

Wa jiigwan gii-wiindmagoon "Nda-mishomis gkendaan aapji emshkoziimgak mashkiki. Gnimaa daa-gkendaan aabziichgan ge-naandwigwod gdaanis. Nga-oo-kwejmaa, miinwaa nga-bskaabii waabang."

Bi-waabang Jiig gii-bipskaabii miinwaa gii-wiindamowaan ninwan gii-gnoonaajin Mishomsan, miinwaa da-mishomsan gii-iiyaanan naaknigewinan waayang. Naaknigewinan gii-aawnoon wii-biinsegin niizhwaaswi mtigoong, takmig eyaasing nikeyaa iw niiwin eyaagamging mtigoong, miinwaa wii-gibaang emtioogmikaak naaknigewin nii'ii wiigwaas nagek. Gii-naaknigegaasa wii-baabii'aad biindik biinish dbikak.

Pii dbikamgak, wa nini gaa-naabi shpiming giizhgoong shiibaayag jiiggamigong. Gii-noondaan ngamwinan miinwaa bemaadzijik giigdowaad enji-bgoneyaag. Gii-maamnanaamaan nangoonsag gchi-gwaabaganan gii-ngwaaminaagziwaad miinwaa niibna waaskonenjiganan gii-bskaaknesenoon giizhgoong. Ninda waaskonenjiganan gii-zhaapsenoon giji bgoneyaag miinwaa gii-maajii-nangse.

Wa nini gii-dbasendam miinwaa gii-nmadabi zhe miinwaa gii-nam'aa. Niwewin gii-wiindmaagoon noojmwoin daansan ge-noojmigod. Gii-wiindmawaan gewe ninwan wii-zhitood maanda nikeyaa gamik pii dowaamdaang naandwewinan maage ngwetmowin pii mnidookaang aki. Eniwewin gii-wiindmogwan wi nini miingoowewzi gii-zhaabwii'aad nooshenhyin bmaadziwini.

Wiiba go, waaskonenjiganan miinwaa nagamwinan gii-ni-pskaapidenoon bgoneyaak gijiying jissgamigong miinwaa gii-bskaabiimgad gchi-gwaabagan. Jichaakok gii-maajiinaawaan Jiigwan shpiming mii dash gii-mi-gweknaagzii'aawaad nangook wi e-zhi-kendaming "jiig-naang."

The man said, "My daughter is very sick and I am trying to make her something nice to wear for the afterlife, but since you're still alive, I will let you go."

The Fisher told him, "My grandfather knows very strong medicine, He may know of the cure that is needed to heal your daughter. I will go ask him and will be back tomorrow."

The next day Fisher came back and told the man that he did speak to his grandfather, and that his grandfather had certain instructions for him. The instructions were to insert seven poles into the ground in a circular position with four rings circling the poles, and to cover this wooded frame with birch bark. He was instructed to wait inside there until nightfall.

When nightfall came, the man looked up at the sky through the opening at the top of the lodge. He could hear singing and people talking through the top of the opening. He noticed that the stars on the big dipper were gone and that many lights were dancing in the sky. These lights came through the top of the lodge and it began to shake.

The man was humbled and sat there and prayed. A voice told him the cure that his daughter was looking for. He also instructed the man to build this kind of lodge when looking for cures or answers from the spirit world. The voice told the man that this was gifted to him for sparing his grandson's life.

Before long, the lights and songs began to fade back through the hole at the top of the lodge and the big dipper was restored. The spirits took Fisher up with them and turned him into stars that we now know as the Little Dipper.

Gchi Odjiik Dbaadjimowin

Gchi-mewzhaa, Giiwednong Ojibwe dbaadtaanaawaa dbaajimowinan wi-gnaagdawendjigaadegin gaa-bi-zhiwebag. Maanda dbaajigaadek gaa-zhiwebag gii-bi naagdawendaanaawaa Gchi-anishinaabek, bebezhig dbaajimowin, daapanind e-bizindang zhezhe'endmowin wii-maanjechgaadek Gchi-mashkiki aabjijgaadek niigaan.

Gchi-anishinaabek noongo giizhgak, kidwag wi gdaawmi wi dbaajimowin, miinwa wi e-niigaanwan waa-bmaadziimgak da-madabiwag giitaayiing shkodeng dbaadamowaad megwaa dbaajmowin nikeyaa 'e-niizhogaadejig' gii-wnaachtoonaaawaa wiinwaa nikeyaa gijitoonaawaa gchi-getin wii-binaachtoowaad Aki.

Ndebwetaan ni mdaaswaak bboongak da dbaadaanaawaa maanda dbaajimowin, maanda megwaa yaayiing.

Great Fisher Story

For centuries, the Northern Ojibwe have been telling stories as a way to keep a record of what has happened in the past. This oral history has been preserved by the Elders, one story at a time, often taking the listener deep into the past to collect the Great Medicine in the story in case it is needed in the future.

The Elders of the present day say that right now we are in a story, and that future generations will be sitting around a fire telling our current story of how the 'two-legged' lost their way and tried to destroy the Earth.

I believe that 1,000 years from now they will be telling this story, the one we are in now.

Aki da'aan nwewin miinwaa enso nooding gnoondaanaa. Gda-noondaanaa wi niwewin pii noondaming wi nibi daangshkang ni siniin. Gda-wiindamaagoonaa gegoo. Wi niwewin gchi-mashkikiimnaan aawan. Miinwa kina ngoji te gaataaaying yaaying.

Gche-nendmojig gdaawmi. Wiinwaa nsastaanaawaa, miinwaa noondaanaawaa wi gchi- giigdowin wenjibaamgak akiing. Wi giigdowin geyaabi te oodi. Geyaabi ga-wiindamaagomi dbaajmowinan gaa-bi-zhiwebag giishpin daapnaming zhisek wii-kendaming.

Dbaajmowinan yaanaawaan Debenjged gaa-miingoying naaknigewinan wi giinwi bemaadzijig waa-mkwendaming miinwaa waa-naagdooying kina gegoo wii-miigsek. 'Tibaabiigsing' aawan bezhig e-ziingaaksiniin wenji kina Ntamsijik e-timaajimowaadgejik. Giinwi gii-gkendaanaa, giinwi nda-gchi-anishinaabejik geyaabi gwiinmaagomi, temigat gchi-naagdwendjigewinan ensa-bemaadziwimgak wii-naagdwendmowaad maanda tibaabiigsewin, miinwaa wenji sanagdingin zhiwebzowinan kina bemaadziimgak akiing pii gaawiin giinwi. Maanda dbaajmowin wa joweyeng giinwi maanda Ninaajewin miinwaa Tibaabiigsewin.

Niibna nsoboongak, Anishnaabek gii-maajiigshinwag waabanong nikeyaa maajaawaad, gii-ni-zhaawag zhaawnong epngishmoog, giiwednong, waabanong. kina nikeyaa eyaaying nongo. Gnoopnadaanaa gchitwaa-miikaans ezhnikaadeg waabano-miikan. Aawan naasaap miikaanhs e-noopnadang giizis, zhaat waabanong biinish epingishmok. Gda-wiindamaagomi niibna nching, gchi-niibna mayegisjig, wii-naagdooying maanda miikaans.

Jibwaa maajikshing gegoo gii-zhiwebad gaa-ni-nji-aanseg kina gegoo. Gegoo gii-zhiwebad gichi-maamkaadenmowin mii go gegaa gii-ngonaagziwaad e-niizhogaadejik maanpii akiing.

The land has a voice and we hear it every time the wind blows. We hear that voice when we hear that water smashing against the rocks. It's telling us something. The voice of the land is Great Medicine for us. And it's everywhere; it surrounds us.

Our people are great philosophers. They understand and hear the great voice that comes from the land. That voice is still out there. It will still tell us the stories of what happened if we take the time to learn.

The stories contain the natural laws which we human beings need to remember and follow in order to keep everything in balance. 'Balance' is one of the cornerstones within all Indigenous philosophies. We know, as our Elders still tell us, there is a great responsibility that each generation has to maintain this balance, and there are severe consequences to all of life on the planet when we don't.

Years ago, the Anishinaabek migrated from East to West, from Wabanong, all the way to where we are now. We were following a very sacred path called Wabano Miikaan. It's the same path that the sun follows, going from East to West. We were instructed many times, by many different beings, to remain on that path.

Before the migration something happened that changed everything. Something happened so profound that it almost wiped off the two-legged from the earth.

Gigkendaan, gdaa'aanaanin gda-shkwaandemnaanin naasmisinoon waabnong nikeyaa. Giizis bi-mookse waabanong nikeyaa miinwaa pii bi-mooksed biindige'aaskone miingoying bmaadziwin. Gdebwetaanaa gda-binoojiinhminaanik nandawendaanaawaa waase'aannhzhewin wii-mna-maajiishkaawaad. Waabanong miikan waabanong biinish epingishmok miikan aawan. Emshkikii'aadzijig geyaabi dbaadaanaawaa. Wesiinyag naagdoonaawaa miikan miinwaa giinwi gii-wiindamaagomi wii-naagdoying wesiinhyag miikaniwaa wii bwaa-bkewdooying.

Gchi-mewnzha Anishinaabek gii-boontaawag naagdoowaad maanda Waabano-miikan. Gii-ni-aanoodziwag. Anishinaabek gii-ndawendaanaawaa bkaan wii-zhinaagoog endaawaad. Gii-maajii-debwetaanaawaa wi wenjishing mshkiki ebi-mookseg bmikwed wesiinh gaawi de-mnik gii-nishshisnoo. Gii-dawendaanaawaa wii-zhitoowaad miikaansan. Mii dash wi gaa-zhigewaad. Gii-zhitoonaawaan miikaansmiwaan.

Eniizhoo-gaadejig nikeyaa gii-naadziwag.

Kino gegoo gii-ni-maanaadse maanda pii. Gaawin eta gii-aanoodzisiiwag, gaawiin gegoo gii-dbaadendasiinaawaa. Baamsewaad gii-baa-boopookbidoonaawaa tikonan. Gii-waabndaanaawaan waawaaskonensan gii-tookaadaanaawaan nishaa. Pii gii-wiisniwaad kina gegoo gii-nshinaajtoonaawaa. Mide gii-pagjigaade ngoji dibishko gaa gegoo aawnsinoog. Gii-bgidnaawaan giigoonhan wii-binaadshinwaad miinwaa kina wesinhan gii-gosigwaan. Eniizho-gaadejig ge'e aakwaapnandiwag. Gii-maajtaawag dzhindiwaad miinwaa gii-bi-zegendaagziwag. Gii-bi-aawag miigaadiiwninwag miinwaa wessinhyag gaawiin gii-gshki'oosiinaawaa wii-ngaabnaawaad.

You know, we have our wigwam doors facing East, and there is a reason for that. It's because the sun rises in the East and when it rises, the light comes into our lodges, giving us life. We believe our children need that light to live and thrive. Wabano Miikaan is that sacred path from East to West that the medicine people still speak about. Animals follow this path, and we were instructed to follow the animal trails so we could remain on this path.

Well, a long time ago the Anishinaabek stopped following this sacred path. They got greedy. The Anishinaabek wanted to have their lodge a different way. They started to believe that the Great Medicine that bursts from animal footprints wasn't good enough. They wanted to make their own trails. And that is what they did. They made their own trails.

They started living life, not like a four-legged, but like a two-legged.

Everything went wrong at this point. Not only did they become very greedy, but they began to disrespect everything. They would just walk along and bust branches when they were walking. They saw flowers and would just step on them for no reason. When they ate, they wasted everything. Fat was just thrown out like it was nothing. They would let fish rot and the Animals were very scared of them. The two-legged also became very mean with one another. They started to talk about each other and become violent. They became very war-like people, and the Animals couldn't stop them.

Gii-gnowaamjige dash wiya kina gegooi e-ni-bi-zhiwebag. Gegoo nooj mechaamigak biinish ee-niizhogaadenid. Gnoowaamjigaaswag shpiming giizhoong, iw giizhgoong.

Mnidoo gii-yaa oodi, nii'sayiing gnoowaabmaad e-niizhogaadejin miinwaa waabmaan e-nokiiwaad, miinwaa aani wnendamowaad wii-noopnadoowaad miikaanhs giw e-niiwogaadejig gaa-zhinoomaagaazwaad.

Maaba mnidoo gii-zhinkaaza Biboon'nini. Kiwenziinh aawi ednizi gchi -giizhgoong, giiwednong. Biboon'nini gii-waabndaan e-zhiwebag miinwaa gii-nendam, "Nga-nsaak e-niizhogaadejig zaam eni-zhi'waad."

Gii-ni-maajtaa boodaajiged niisaying kiing da-gchitwaa nesewin miinwaa kina gegoo gii-maajii-mashkowaakidini.

Zaam dash, gii-temigad mashkiki maanpii akiing nooj emshkooziimmigak wiin dash da-nesewin.

Mii dash gii bneshiinyag.

Pii bneshiinyag ngamwaad gchitwaa nagamwinan gii-bskaabigaanjwebnaanaawaa doo nesewininim. Gchi-niibna mishkiki teni bneshiinhyag ngamwinwaan ge'e wii-gaanjwebshkimowaad getin neyaap Biboon'nini doo-nesewin. Kiwenziinh gii-gkendaan wi wiin da-mashkoziiwin gaawiin gii-mashkoziimgasnoo biinish ne'end bineshiinhag doo-nagamwinwaan.

Mii sa gii-nendang gegoo ge-zhichgepa.

But, there was somebody watching all that was happening. Someone who was bigger than the two-legged. They were being watched from above, from the sky. A spirit was up there, looking down at the two-legged and seeing how they were acting, and how they had forgotten to follow the path the four-legged had showed them.

This spirit's name is Biboon'nini. He is the Old Man that lives way up in the universe, in the North. Biboon'nini saw what was happening and he thought to himself, 'I'm going to destroy the two-legged for how they are acting.'

So he began to blow down onto earth with his sacred breath and everything started to freeze.

But, there was a medicine here on earth that was stronger than his breath.

It was the Birds.

When the Birds sang their sacred songs it pushed his cold breath back. There is so much medicine in the Bird's songs that they pushed back Biboon'nini's breath with great force. The Old Man knew that his power wasn't as strong as those sacred songs the Birds were singing.

So he got an idea.

Gii-nendaan, "Nga-ni-zhaa niisaying aki miinwaa nga-maandooshmaak kina bineshiinyag miinwaa nga-tkobnaak maamwi biinjiyiing gchi-shkimdaang. Nga-maajiinaak nda-wiigwaaming enji-nangoonskaak. Miinwa dash nga-nesendwag." Mii dash gaa-zhichged. Gii-maawndooshmaan kina bneshiinyan miinwaa boodaadaan da-mkomii-dekaak nesewin.

Aki gii-maajii-nboodewzi zaam ngamwinan gii-ngonaagdoon. Miinwaa gaa-wiindamowin, mii go wewiib gii-mashkowaakdin ki. Wa kiwenziinh gii-boodaajge da-gchitwaa-nesewin gchigetin kina gegoo gii-maajii-mashkowaakdin miinwaa nibagashnad.

Anishnaabek zhaazhi ko gaawiin gii-niimsiiwag zaam giiwnishnoog. Gaawiin gkendaziinwaawaa waa-zhichigewaad miinwaa ooshme gii-aanoodziwag, zaagtoonaawaa miijim miinwaa zaagziwag. Wesiinyag dash gii-maajii-maawnjidiwag miinwaa gii-yaawaanaawaa naaknigewinkeng. Gii-maajtaawag wii-nam'aawaad miinwaa ngamwaad miinwaa kwedwewag zhinoomaagewin miinwaa naadmaagewinan. Gii-bgidnaawaan semaan gaa-bwaanootooying wii-bgidnaayiing.

Wa e-gaachiinhid wesiinh kida, "Kaa, te go zhaabwiiwin. Aabdek kwii-gjitoonaa maanda eyaawang. Gaa maamda wii-boontaaying."

Jiig gii-bgdinaan da-semaaman ntam, mii dash gii-giigdad. Ngwisenhsim endaayaan ngii-wiindmaak temigad ezhichigengoba. Nda-binoojiinhyim ngii-wiindmaak waaboowaan gaawiin nokiimgasnoo. Ki Odeng ndoo-ndinaan mshkoziiwin miinwaa giizhoozwin, temigat go zhichigewin.

He thought to himself, 'I'm going to go down to earth and I'm going to collect all those Birds and I'm going to tie them up in a great big bag. I'll take them up to my wigwam in the stars. And then I'll blow my breath.' So, that is what he did. He collected all the Birds and blew his ice cold breath.

The earth became so lonely because the songs were gone. The earth froze quickly. That Old Man blew his sacred breath so hard that everything started to freeze and perish.

The Anishinaabek were already very weak because they had lost their way. They didn't know what to do and began to become more greedy, hoarding their food and being stingy. But the Animals started to gather and have meetings. They started to pray and sing and ask for guidance and help. They were the ones that were putting their tobacco down when the Anishinaabek couldn't.

At one of these meetings, the Animals all lost hope except for one little Animal, the Odjig, the Fisher. That little Animal said, "No, there has to be a way. We have to try to figure this out. We cannot give up."

Fisher put his tobacco down first and then spoke, "My little son at home told me that there is a way. My child told me that his blanket that he wrapped around him is not working and that he gets his strength and his warmth from the heartbeat of the land. There is a way."

Aadash aabdek pii gii-bdaajigaadek wi nikeyaa, kina gii-gkendaanaawaa wiindmaagewin wa Ojiigoonhs gaa-miigwed geget gii-biinaagot gchitwaa-mshkiki gaa-dingaadek. Gii-gkendaanaawaa gegoo ge-zhichgewaapa wii-ngaabjigaazod wa kiwenziinh wii-booninesendangaki.

Mii sa gii-bgidnaawaad seaman. Miinwa gii-giishaaknigewag wii-kwaandwewaad shpaabkaak. Ngoding gaa-dgoshinawaad gidaabik, gii-aanjgwashkniwag nangwang aa'aankaaj. Mii dash gii biindigewaad keweziinh endaad nasal gii bneshiinhag, giimooj, ka-bskaabwenag aking, da-newninaawaa da-mashkiki miinwaa iw bemaadiiwin mibdek wii-shaabwiiyaad bemaadzijik - naasaap e-niiwogaadejik, miinwaa e-niizhogaadejik. Gii-gkendaanaawaa wii-zhaawaad oodi miinwaa wii-gijitoowaad wii-ginoonaawaad kiwenziinhyan. Nishin naaknigewin gaa-naaknigewaad.

Kina e-nishing naaknigewin maajtaamigad gegoo nwewesing. Maajtaamigad wenji-makadewaamigak. Pii dash niwewin zhichigaadek, mibdemigad miinwaa dawaamdaan iw mshkiki endowaamdamek. Wesiinhyag gkendaanaawaa mii manad nikeyaa ezhi-bmaadziwaad.

Well of course when it was explained like that, they all knew that the message the little Fisher gave was very pure, it held great medicine. They knew that they had to come up with a way to stop the Old Man from blowing his breath down on earth.

So, they too put their tobacco down. And what was agreed upon was that they were going to climb a high mountain. Once they were up on the mountain they would jump up from star to star and they would go into that Old Man's wigwam, grab the Birds, sneak them out and bring them back to earth so that their voice, their medicine and the life they carry will save the people—both the four-legged, and the two-legged. They knew they had to go up there and try to negotiate with the Old Man. That was the plan and it was a good plan.

Every good plan starts with a sound. It starts from black. Once the sound is made, it travels and seeks the medicine that you are looking for. The Animals know this and live by it.

Mii dash wi gaa-zhichgewaad. Gii-ngamwag dash wii-mkigaadek aakdewin miinwaa mashkoziiwin waa-meneswaad waa-zhaawaad Waadese dowaamjigewin wii-zhaabwiitoowaad aki.

Kina gegoo gii-mashkowaakdin.

Wa kiwenziinh gaawiikaa gii-naagdawenmaasiin e-niizhogaadejig. Wiin eta gii-boodaajige, boodaajige, boodaajige.

Niiwin wesiinhag gii-nendamook wii-zhaawaad. Gaak wiintam wesiinh ndawendaan wii-zhaat. Gaawiin daa-gshkitoosiin gdinendam. Gaak daa'aan emshkoziimgak bakwan. Miinwaa gaak daa'aan emshkoziimgak ode.

Nigig aawi eko-niishing wesiinh waa-zhaad meshkoziid miinwaa emshkowsiimgak mashkiim. Gaawiin gegoo tesnoo Ngig ge-maashigopa.

Wa Bizhiw dash gewiin gii-ndawendaan wii-zhaad, "Ndaa-zhichige go maanda," gii-kida. "Nda-aanan emshkoziimgakin kaatdan, nda-bagwaashkin gchi-shpiming miinwaa nda-gwaashkwes.

Miinwaa dash eko-niiwing wesiinh gii-aawi Jiig, gchitwaa-jiig.

Wiinwaa giw e-niiwogaadejig gii-daapinigaaswok gchi-maandawin kiing wii-zhaawaad shpiming wii-zhaabwiitoowaad aki. E-niizhogaadejig gii-maajii-aakoziwag.

Gaa-dgoshnowaad gidaabik gii-mshkozii'aadziwag. Gii-gkendaanaawaa kina gegoo giizhiitaamgak weweni zhaazhi go. Wa semaa gii-bgidnigaasa. Ngamwinan gii-ngamwag. Waamjigewin wa eshkiniigid miinwa mdawemgak gaa-dbaadang gii-te da-nendmowininwaang.

So that is what they did. They sang their songs in order to find the courage and strength that they would need to go on their warrior's quest to save the world.

Everything was frozen solid.

The Old Man never pitied the two-legged. He just kept blowing and blowing and blowing.

Four Animals decided to go. The first animal that wanted to go was the Gaak, the Porcupine. A very unlikely hero when you think about it. The Porcupine has a strong back. And Porcupine has a strong heart.

The second animal that wanted to go was the Nigig, the Otter and he is very fierce. He is a warrior and their medicine is strong. There are not too many things that can beat up an Otter.

The other animal that chose to go was the Bizhew, the Lynx. "I can do this," he said, "I have strong legs, I can jump high, and I'm quick."

And of course, the fourth animal was Odjig, the Great Fisher.

Those were the four that were chosen by the great mystery of this land to go up there to save the earth. The two-legged began to perish.

When they got up to the mountain, they felt strong. They knew everything was done correctly beforehand. The tobacco was put down. The songs had been sung. The vision of that young person and heartbeat he talked about was in their minds.

Gii-naaknigewag. Gii-kidwag, "Ka-debinaanaa Gaak nikaang miinwaa kaading miinwa ga biimskwaashmaanaa miinwaa gabawebnaa'naa zaam gaawiin ntaa-jigwaashkinisii."

Mii sa gaa-zhichigewaad. Getin gii-bagwebnaawaan. Dash pii gii-ni-biimskwaashing zhi, gii-bsikaan gegoo. Gegoo ewaamdasgwaa.

Te gchi-mashkoziiwin, kiinwi gda-waamdaziinaa dash wii go temigad.

Gaawiin gii-zhaabisiiwag.

Gaak gii-bagojin zhe'e miinwaa gii-bskaabaashi neyaap akiing giji aazhbikoong. Pii gaag dagojing shkweyaang kaadan giitkokiiseni miinwaa gii-bookshkaani kaadan miinwaa gii-nitipijiise aazhbikoong.

Mii dash jida Gaagoog enji-zhinaagziwaad nongo. Shashwejiisewag. Pii waabdmadwaa, dibishko shkweyaang zidaawaang bookshkaanik shawegaadesiwag. Maanda dash wii-mjimendaming wi pii gii-aawang e-niizhogaadejig giiaanoodziwaad miinwaa wii-gimaakdaanaawaa aki.

Ngig dash gii-dawendaan wiintam wii-njigwashknid. Ngig giigchi-bagowaashkini getin. Miinwaa pii Ngig gii-bagwaashkinid, wiin go ge gii-btaakshkaan wi mashkoziiwin miinwaa giibi-niisgojin kiing. Miinwaa pii Ngig daangshkang aki, giipangdagojin shiwedaaki gii-ni-shooskbizo niisaaki.mii wi Ngig enji-zhooshkjiwed wi nikeyaa nongo. Gwii-maamnanendaamin e-niizhogaadeying gaa-zhiwebak pii bzindowaasiiying Gashnaa, aki.

They made a plan. They said, "We'll grab Porcupine by his arms and legs and we'll swing him and throw him up because he's not a good jumper."

So, they did that. They threw him up, hard. But when he went spiraling up there, before he could reach the stars, he hit something. It was something that they couldn't see.

There is a great power we can't see but it is there.

He couldn't go through it.

Porcupine just bounced right off of it and came shooting back down to earth onto the mountain. When he landed, he landed on his back feet, and busted them and went rolling down the mountain.

That is why porcupines are like that today. They wobble. When you see them it's like their back feet are busted, they are off to the side and are swollen. This is to remind us of that time when the two-legged became very greedy and wanted to rule the earth.

The next one that wanted to do the jump was Otter, Nigig. Nigig took that big leap, and hard. And when Nigig jumped up, he too hit that power before he could reach the stars and came smashing down to earth. And when Nigig hit the earth, he landed on the side of the mountain and slid all the way down. That is why otters slide around like that today. It's to remind us two-legged of what happened when we didn't listen to our mother, the earth.

Bizhiw dash minwaa wiintam. Bizhiw mashkozii. Jepzii. Miinwaa gii-gkendaasa. E-maanenjget aawi. Gii-nendam, 'aabdek kwii-zhichgemi maanda. Aabdek wii-shaapseying. Giishpin zhaapseswang kina ga-shkwaasemi.'

Mii sa gii-bagwaashkinit bizhiw. Getin. Miinwaa pii Bizhiw gii-ptaakshkaang giizhgoong, gewii go gii-bagishing neyaap akiing. Gii-miikowaan nook getin biinish giiyek niizh zaam gii-gchi-bgosendam. Gii-gchi-bgosendam kina etek akiing wii-bmaadziimgag. Gii-gchi-bgosendam wii-gnawendmang bemwidooying gde'enaan.

Pii bizhiw gaa-ndagoojing gidaazhbik, gii-pangshin enji-giinaak miinwaa gii-giizhkseni zowaanag. Mii wi njida bizhiw nongo tkwaanwed miinwaa enji-zhinaagzid gii-bagajiishgaadenik wdengwe. Wii-maamnanendaming gaa-zhiwebag pii e-niizhogaadejig gii-nendmowaad wii-naagdoowaad da-miikanmiwaa miinwaa wii-mnaadendaziiwaad kina gegoo.

Ojiig eta gaa-yaad nshike geyaabi oodi shpiming. Gii-nboodewzi miinwa gii-zhiyaa gii-maachigaaza zaam wiijkenyin gii-maajaawag. Gii-zhiyaa dibishko gaawiin gii-yaasiin mashkoziiwin wii-zhichiged zaam giiyek aanind nswi nooj gii-mashkoziiwag gichitaag miinwaa gaawiin gkendaziin waa-zhichiged. Gaa-makwendaang eta gwisan. Miinwaa gii-makwendamaad gwisan, gii-nendam wi mshkowendmowin miinwa bagosendmowin gwisan gaa-mwiwdood.

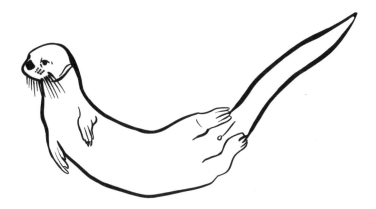

The next animal was Bizhew, the Lynx. Bizhew is strong. He's quick. He's smart. He is a warrior. He thought, 'we have to do this. We have to get through. If we don't get through everything will perish.'

So Bizhew jumped. Hard. And when Bizhew hit that power called Giizhikdong, he too came smashing back down to earth. He hit it harder than the other two because he was desperate. He was desperate for all the life to live that was on the earth. He was desperate to keep the heartbeat alive that we all carry.

When Bizhew landed on the mountain, he landed on a sharp rock and he busted his tail off. That is why Bizhew today has a short tail and why he looks like his face is smashed in. It's to remind us of what happened when the two-legged decided to follow their own path and disrespect everything.

The only one that was left up there all alone was Fisher, Odjig. He felt lonely and he felt defeated because his friends were gone. He felt like maybe he didn't have the strength to do it because those other three were very strong warriors and he didn't know what to do. All he thought about was his son. And when he thought about his son, he thought about the faith and hope his son carried.

Gii mkendaan gchi gitsiiman gaa kinoomaagwad. Gii naandoojiinge naami goon, gii mkaanan ngodwaaswi miinan. Gii bgidnaan da semaman, miinwaa miinan gii dgosdoonan. Pii gaa daatgikwenad. Gegoo gii-waabndaan! Gii-waabndaan gegoo gaa-miinid kina bgosendmowin maanpii akiing. Gii-waabndaan bgoneyaag giizhgoong aanipii aanind wesiinhag gii-bkiteshnowaad. Gii-gkendaan wi giishpin gii-ni-aabjitaad gojitood wii-ni-zhaabizad. Mii go wewiib gii-gkendang wii-zhichiged maanda.

Gii-bagwaashkni dash. Miinwa gii-bagwaashkni miinwaa. Miinwaa. Miinwaa. Miinwaa.

Gaawiin gii-boontaasii biinish gegpii gii-dpibsod.

Pii gii-zhaabgwaashknid, gaa yaa yaawaad nangook. Gii-naabi nikeyaa wa kiwenziinh ednizid.

Gii-yaa gchi-jijaak ekowaamdang shkwaandem wa kizwenziinh endaad. Jijaak daa'aan niwewin enoondming gchi-waasa. Miinwaa biigwe-emgad.

Giishpin wiikaa gii-noondaman ewiisgwiweg da-nwewin jijaak gdaa-biimskogaabow miinwaa gdaa-gwekgaabow. Jiig gii-gkendaan temgak gchi-maanenjigewin.

Odjig remembered what his grandparents had taught him. He dug around under the snow and found six bear berries. He grabbed his tobacco and he laid it down with the offerings of the berries and when he looked up, he saw something! He saw something that gave him all the hope in the world. He saw a crack in Giizhikdong where the other Animals hit. He knew that if he kept trying that he could bust his way through, and he knew in that moment that he had to do this.

So, he jumped. And he jumped again. And again. Again.

He didn't stop jumping until he finally busted through.

And when he busted through he found himself in the star world. He looked to where that Old Man lived.

There was a great big Crane guarding the doorway of the Old Man's wigwam. A crane has a voice that can be heard for miles. And they are loud!

If you have ever heard the shrilling voice of a crane there is a very good chance you will turn around and go the other way. So, Fisher knew he had a big challenge in front of him.

Dash miinwaa gii-bgidnaan da-semaaman. Gaa-nendang dash, "Aabdek nwi-bskaabii neyaap niiseying biwaad mtigook. Aabdek nii-maawnjaa gaawaandgo bgiw. Aabdek nwii-daapnaan gaawaandago-bgiw miinwaa nga-ni-giimoodis yaad jijaak miinwaa gshkamoonaa-bigewan pii gaanjwebnag wa gaawaandgo-bgiw dooning gnabaj gaawiin da-gshkitoosiin wii-biigzid giishpin gaanjwebnag de-mnik dooning."

Mii wi da-naaknigewin miinwaa gii-aawan e-nishing naaknigewin.

Mii dash wi gaa-zhichiged. Gii-ni-moode niiseying akiing miinwaa gii-maajtaa wii-maawnjiaad gaawaandgo-bgiwan. "Aah shkenaa! Gnandawenmin. Gii-naan mtigoong." Gii-kida, "Nandwendaan wii-zhichigeyaan maanda. Nandwendaan aanind ji-daapnag. Nanwendaan ji-naadmooyin. Daga! Bangii eta nandwendaan." Miinwaa gii-maawnjiaad gaawaandgo-bgiwan biinish gii-yang ngod-ninj mii dash gii-ni-bskaabiid neyaap zhi enji-bgoneyaak.

Shpiming gaa-dgoshing gii-maajii-gimoodzi nangoong gii-ni'aa'aanjii. Gegpii gii-ni-yaa besha jijaak yaad. Kina gegoo gaa-zhaamgak maanpii. Gii-gkendaan 'mii maanda aawang.'

Dash gii-saan da-semaaman nangoong miinwaa gii-ni-zhaa wiigwaaming. Jijaak gii-waabmaan. Miinwaa go wewiip gii-waabmigwod jijaakoon, gii-bakdoonnewi da-gchi-doon miinwaa gaa zhichiged wi ojiig gii-biinjwebnaan gaawaandgo-bgiw biinji gowandaagnining. Jibwaa ni-pidek dash neyaap kina, jijak gii-nwe bangii, "ga!" Mii maanda gaa-noondang kiwenziinh mii dash gii-naajbatwaanaad bkwaakoon.

Gchi-maandaa pkwaakoon gii-aawnoon wa kiwenziinh gaa-yaangin. Daa-pidenoon ekwaayiing kiing, mii epiichi gwek miikogemgag.

So again, he put down his tobacco. What he thought was, 'I need to go back down to where the trees are. I need to collect some spruce gum, gowaandak-bigew. And I need to grab spruce gum and sneak back up to where the Crane is and shove it in his mouth...when I shove that spruce gum in his mouth maybe he won't be able to make that loud noise if I jam it in there far enough.'

That was his plan. And it was a good plan.

So, that is what he did. He crawled down to earth through that hole in Giizhikdong and he started to collect spruce gum. "Oh please! I need you!" He said to the tree. "I need to take some. I need to do this. I need your help. Please! I just need a little bit." And he collected the spruce gum until he had a nice good handful of it and then went back up through that hole.

Once up, he snuck from star to star to star. Finally, he was getting close to where the Crane was. Everything had led up to this very moment. He knew, 'This is it!'

He put down his tobacco on a star and he charged for the wigwam. Crane saw him. As soon as Crane saw him, he opened up his great big mouth and just as he did, Fisher rammed the spruce gum down his throat. But just before it got all the way back, Crane made a little gawking noise, "Ga!" That little sound was enough for the Old Man to start running for his arrows.

The Old Man's arrows are not like regular arrows. They are magic arrows. They could go to the end of the earth to find their mark no problem.

Ojiig gii-mookiitaanan wiigwaam. Gii-ni-debnaan bneshiinhyan gii-ni-zaagjibtwanaan. Wewiib gii-maajiibmiptood wiiji bneshiinyan neyaap oodi tek enji-bgoneyaak giizhigoong nikeyaa.

Gaawiin waasa gii-patoosii pii gii-noondang wi. Enwe'esing mtigowaab gii-aawan. Gii-gkendaan wi mtigwaab biijbideg shkweyaang yaad. Mii gwa eta enendang neyaap wii-bskaabwebnaad bgoneyaag biw bineshiinhan.

Mii gwa gewiin naasaap engwakwaak win go mshkimat bineshiinhag. Gii gkendaan giishpin wii dpinaad niw bineshiinhan, gaawiin wii-debshkinesii geyii. Mii dowaach gii-gwetaanbatod. Jiig gii-debwetang daa-gshkitoon.

Pii Jiig e-ni-dgoshing enji-bgoneyaag, gii-debidoon wi ngodooshkin bineshiinhag miinwa tpaawebnaan enji-bgoneyaag epiichibawed gaawiin gii-zhisesii wii-niisgwaashknid. Gii-aabjibtoo, miinwaa mtigwaabiin gii-miikogaazo.

Mtigwaabiin gii-baataashnini maa zhingishing. Gii-saasaakwe gii-gshkitood. Gii-gkendaan bneshiinyag miinwaa gchitwaa nagamwinan emiwdoowaad da-biidoonaawaa gchitwaa-mshkikiin kina akiing. Gii-gkendaan tek geyaabi waaseyaandmowin. Gii-nsastaan dash, wi aawang bemadood miikan wii-nbod nji bemdaadzijik. Miinwaa mii dash go miyaa gaa-zhichiged.

Gii-gchinendam dash wa kiwenziinh gii-nsaad jiigwan. Zaam mii wa gaa-gchi-maanenmigojin wi pii. Jiig ooshme gaa-gchi-maanenmigojin. Miinwaa wa kiwenziinh gii-gkendaan aabdek waa-zhichiged eta wii-bskaabiid akiing wii-maawnjiwebnaad giw ngo mshkimod bneshiinhag miinwaa neyaap gii-zaan wiigwaaming miinwaa gii-boodajge doo-gchitwaa-nesewin. Dibishko go naa gaawiin gegoo wiikaa gii-zhiwebsinoog.

Fisher charged into the wigwam, grabbed the Birds and sped out. Quickly he started running with the Birds back to where that hole in Giizhikdong was.

He hadn't run very far when he heard it. It was the snap of the Old Man's bow string. He knew the arrow was coming behind him and all he could think about was getting those Birds down through that hole.

Now, the size of the hole and the size of the bag of Birds was the same. He knew if he was going to get those Birds down that hole, he wouldn't be able to go down the hole himself. That made him run harder and faster. It made Fisher believe that he could do it.

When Fisher got to the hole, he grabbed the bag of Birds and put it down into the hole as he just kept travelling over it. He didn't have time to jump down. He kept running, and that's when he got shot with the arrow.

He lay there with the arrow stuck in him and cried with great joy because he did it! He knew that the Birds and the sacred songs that they carried were going to bring Great Medicine across the land and melt all the ice. He knew there was still hope! He understood then, that that was part of his journey, to die for the people. And that is exactly what he did.

Of course, the Old Man was happy he killed Fisher because that was his greatest enemy at that time. Fisher had been the greatest one yet to challenge him. And the Old Man knew that all he had to do was just go back down to earth to gather those Birds back up in a bag and put them back in his wigwam and blow his sacred breath. Just like nothing had happened.

Pii Jiig epiichi-nibowad shpiming oodi, gegoo gii-zhiwebad. Pii gii-shkwaanaamod, "haaaaaaaaah," wi nesewin gii-mibdemigad baandowaamndang mshkiki. Dibishko kiinwi gda-namewininaa miinwaa gbmaadziwininaa ni-aapjiibde shkwaa naamyiing. Da-chitwaa-nesewin gii-mewidoon kwedwewin gaa-mibdek miiyaa waa-ni-zhaamgak.

Gii-yaawag ngodwaaswi mnidook miindawaa gaa-gchitwaa kwedwein wi gaa-bgidnigaadek shkwaa naamoong. Giw mnidook gii-waamdaanaawaa kina gegoo. Ntam dash gaawiin gii-baamendmaasiiwaan wa kiwenziinh waa-zhichigenid. Aanii dash? E-niizhoogaadejig gii-bi-bnaachtoonaawaa kina gegoo. Gaa-shkwaa-waamdamowaad Jiig aakdewin, gii-nagaawendmaawaan e-niiwogaadenindjin. Giw ngodwaaswi mnidook gii-bi-zhaawag wa kiwenziinh endaad. Gii-wiidabimaawaan miinwaa gii-maajtaawag gnoonaawaad. Gmaamnanendaan na Jiig gii-dawendaan wii-zhichiged wi. Gii-dawendaan wii-dbaaknigewaad miinwaa wii-gnoonaad ni kiwenziinhyan.

Da-nesewin, da-shkwaach-naamwin gii-gchi-aawan go gegoo.

Giw ngodwaaswi mnidook gaa-nbwaachaawaad niw kiwenziinhan endaanid gii-wiindamaagwaan. "Ndoo-mnaadendaanaa ezhichigeyin. Ndoo-mnaadendaanaa wgojitooyin wii-biinaagoog aki e-niizhogaadejig gaa-zhichigewaad. Kii mshkoowaakjimang wesiinhag, gaawiin wesiiyag gegoo gii zhichgesewag, miinwaa kii ntoonan ezaakiigin, kii gmoodnag bineshiinhag, gaawiin maanda gii nishizinoon. Waaseyaandmowin ngii-waamdaamin. Gaa-waamdamaang gchi-shkiki eswesing mzawe kiing. Gegoo gwa nendaagwod. Aapta eta gnesewin kaboodaajge. Ndebwetaanaa debwemigad ezhichigeyin. Ndoo-dawendaanaa ge bineshiinyag ji-ngamtaanaawaa ninda gchitwaa-ngamwinan. Nda-debwetaanaa ezhichigewaad giw gewiinwaa."

But when Fisher was dying up there, something did happen. When he gave his last breath, "Haaaaaaaaah," that breath travelled seeking medicine, just like our prayers and life keeps travelling long after we're gone. His sacred breath carried a request that travelled exactly to where it needed to go.

There were Six Spirits that received his sacred petition, that was offered through his last breath. Those spirits had also seen everything. At first, they didn't intervene with what the Old Man was trying to do. Why would they? The two-legged really destroyed everything. But after seeing the strong courage of Odjig, they pitied the four-legged. The Six Spirits came travelling to where that Old Man's wigwam was. They sat with him and started to talk with him. Remember Fisher wanted to do that? He wanted to negotiate and talk with the Old Man.

His breath, his very last breath had really meant something.

Those Six Spirits that visited the Old Man in his lodge told him, "We respect what you're trying to do. We respect that you are trying to cleanse the earth of the two-legged for what they have done. But you were also freezing the Animals and it wasn't their fault, and you were killing all the plants and you kidnapped all the Birds and that was not right. What we have seen is hope. What we've seen is Great Medicine being cast around the earth. And it means something. What we would like to see is you blow your breath for half the time. Because we believe what you are doing is true. But we also want to let Birds sing their sacred songs for half the time. Because we believe in what they do too."

Megwaa dash nongo ezhi-gkendmang bboon miinwaa niibin gaa-zhi-zhichigaadek. Pii mnookmig, mii pii gshkakmikwe mooshkang. Biijgaade mshkiki pii ngamwaad bineshiinhag kina ngoji akiing.

Ga-waabndaan gchi-gwaabigan pii mnookmik. Giw ngodwaaswi mnidook shpimiing eyaajig gii-kidwag, "wii-mjimedman jiig gaa-zhichiged, odeh wii-mjimendman, nangoonhsing ka-zhi'aanaa maaba Jiig."

Mii sa gchi-gwaabigan gii-zhi'aanjaawaa Jiigwan. Da-mii'aawsin gchi-gwaabigan mnookmig. Mii maanda bmaadziwin edming. Pii mii'aawsing wii-gmiwan. Nibi bi-zhaabgaa, bgonegiizhik-maampii bmaadziwin wii-tek mii maanda gaa-nji-zhitoowaad Bgonegiizhik giw e-niiwoogaadejig. Wi gchitwaa nibi biidaajwan wii-maajigooyiing, miinwaa kina gegoo bi-aabziimgak, maadwe'esdoonaawaa egaachiinhjig akiing.

Pii dash dgwaagik, gchi-gwaabigan namkosin, miinwaa mskwi mijiiwan aapii gaa-nikoonin mtigwaab gii-nakaasang. Mskwiaanswan kina mtigoon. Da maajtaamigad bboon pii nesendang. Gaagge bmaadziwin miinwaa nbowin da biimskobde.

Mnookmik miinwaa dgwaagik, gaa-zhiwebakiba, gchi-gwaabigan gmikwenmaanaa pii e-niizhogaadejig gii-wnishniwaad. Pii mkwendmaanh wi dbaajimowin, nda-makwendaan nongo miinwaa geget ndebwetaan waa-ni-zhiwebak da-dbaadaanaawaa e-zhiwebak megwaa. Miinwaa gbanaj kiinwi, aabdek e-niizhogaadejig da-bigwaashkniwag wii-niigaaniiwaad. Geget nangoonhsan wii-debnaawaad. Gnabaj e-niizhogaadejig da-daapnanaawaa bgosendmowin. E-niizhoogaadeying aabdek gwii-mkaanaa miikan miinwaa. Aabdek kwii-mkaanaa wi gchitwaa-miikaanhs e-piddemgak wabanong nikeyaa biinish epingishmok nikeyaa. Aabdek kwii-mkwaanaa gchitwaa-mshkiki e-baashjiishkaak mikwewaad e-niiwogaadejig.

Of course, at that very instant, that is what became winter and summer as we know it. In the springtime, when mother earth's water breaks, those Birds sound their sacred songs to the world and bring medicine to everything.

You'll also notice a set of stars in the springtime. Those Six Spirits up there said, "To commemorate what Fisher did, to commemorate his heart, we are going to turn Fisher into stars."

So, they turned Fisher into the Big Dipper. In the spring time you'll see the Big Dipper upright, this represents life. When it's upright, the water breaks. Water comes through the 'sacred hoop,' Bgonegiizhik—the hole in Giizhikdong that the four-legged made so that life here could flourish. That sacred water comes and gives us life and the sound of life is then cast out into the world through our little ones.

Then in the fall, the Big Dipper goes upside down and blood will run from where it got shot from that arrow. The blood paints all of our trees red. And then the Old Man will blow his breath and winter will begin. The cycle of life and death continues.

Both in the spring and in fall, the Big Dipper is to remind us of what happened when the two-legged lost their way. When I think about that story, I think about now and truly believe that in the future, they are going to be talking about what happened right now. And maybe us, the two-legged have to be the ones to make that jump and reach for the stars. Maybe it's the two-legged that have to take that leap of faith. As two-legged, we have to find that trail again. We have to find that sacred path that goes from East to West. We have to find the Great Medicine that is bursting out of the foot prints of the four-legged relatives.

Niibna bemaazdzijik da-kidwag wegnesh maanda edming? Mii maanda ezhi-nsastamaanh neyaap wii-daapendmang wii-daaying kiing. Wii-kendaming gda-niwewin'naa. Nsastaagwod wii-bskaabiiying kiing miinwa wii-zhigeying wiigwaaman wii-zhitooying. Dbaajmowin nongo dewendaagwod nooj geyaabi. Dawendaagod go maanda wii-giishaajmoying. Mii dash gzondeheshkoon wii-bigwashkniyin. Bigwashknin, gdi-bendaagozimin dbaajmowining.

Gaawiin gegoo aawzinoo enokiiying nendaagod. Ka-gwekwendamoin giishpin mashko-bakwanesiigoban gaak giishpin bwaa-mshkogaadepan bizhiw, miinwaa meshkodehed ngig. Jiig kaa daa-gii-gshkitooslin wii-zhaapsed.

Kina gegoo ezhichigeying nongo, da-gchi-nendaagod waa-ni-zhiwebag.

A lot of people will say: What does that mean? To me it means getting back to the land. It means learning our language. It means getting back to the land and building those wigwams. The story now needs that more than ever. Our story now is depending on that. And so, I encourage you to take that leap. I encourage you to take that jump because we are in the story now.

Maybe the work that we do now doesn't seem like it means anything. But I'll guarantee you, if it wasn't for the strong back of Porcupine, if it wasn't for the strong legs of Bizhew the Lynx, and the strong heart of Nigig the Otter, Fisher never would have made it through.

Everything that we do now is going to matter in the future.

The Trail of Nenaboozhoo
and Other Creation Stories

ABOUT THE AUTHOR

Photo credit: Alex Usquiano

Bomgiizhik (Isaac Murdoch) is from Serpent River First Nation located on Anishinaabek Territory on the North Shore of Lake Huron. He has spent many years on the land as a hunter, trapper, and fisherman. During these years, he became infatuated with Ojibwe symbolism and began a life long journey of researching pictographs and sacred sites. He currently lives at Nimkii Aazhibikoong and has a beautiful daughter named Waabigwan.

ABOUT THE EDITOR

Christi Belcourt is a renowned Michif (Métis) visual artist with a deep respect for Mother Earth, the traditions and the knowledge of her people. Christi's work is found within the permanent collections of the National Gallery of Canada, the Art Gallery of Ontario, Gabriel Dumont Institute, Parliament Hill and many more. In addition to the arts, she is also respected as a grassroots leader, environmentalist and advocate for the lands, waters and Indigenous peoples. She and Isaac Murdoch form the Onaman Collective which focuses on collaboration, art, resurgence of language and revitalization of land-based traditional arts practices. Together, with others, they built Nimkii Aazhbikoong, a year round language and traditional camp for Youth and Elders. She is author of **Medicines To Help Us** (Gabriel Dumont Institute, 2007) and **Beadwork** (Ningwakwe Learning Press, 2010) and co-editor of **Keetsahnak** (University of Alberta Press, 2018).